BAD SEAMEN!

The three men Moses was tussling with were seamen by appearance. None of them seemed to be wearing gun belts, but they were all brandishing knives, as was Moses. A good seaman always carried a knife, and knew how to do many things with it—of which killing was just one.

Clint decided not to wade in but to use his gun to dissuade the men from continuing their attack. He drew and fired into the air twice, attracting their attention.

However, instead of breaking off the attack, one of the men shouted, "I'll take him," and pulled a gun from his belt . . .

THE GUNSMITH

185

THE BILOXI QUEEN

J. R. ROBERTS

J

JOVE BOOKS, NEW YORK

THE BILOXI QUEEN

A Jove Book / published by arrangement with
the author

PRINTING HISTORY
Jove edition / May 1997

The Putnam Berkley World Wide Web site address is
http://www.berkley.com

ISBN: 0-515-12071-5

A JOVE BOOK®
Jove Books are published by The Berkley Publishing Group,
200 Madison Avenue, New York, New York 10016.
JOVE and the "J" design are trademarks
belonging to Jove Publications, Inc.

PRINTED IN THE UNITED STATES OF AMERICA

10 9 8 7 6 5 4 3 2 1

ONE

Clint Adams rode into Biloxi, Mississippi, with a great sense of anticipation. He had been on riverboats before, and always enjoyed himself. Usually the boat was owned by his friend J. P. Moses, and this one was no exception. Moses had written to him in Labyrinth, telling him about his new boat, the *Biloxi Queen*. He invited Clint to come to Biloxi for the inaugural cruise, which would take them from Biloxi to New Orleans by way of the Mississippi Delta, and then up to St. Paul, in Minnesota. Along the way there would be a lot of food, drink, music, women, and gambling—all of which were things that Clint truly enjoyed indulging in.

Clint arrived the day before the boat was set to leave Biloxi for New Orleans, so he saw that Duke was tended to in a livery stable and then got himself a hotel room for the night. That done he went to get himself a drink and a meal. After that he'd go down to the dock to see the *Biloxi Queen*, and his friend, the famed riverboat gambler J. P. Moses. Moses had a reputation on the Mississippi that almost rivaled Clint's reputation in the West.

The very first settlement ever built in Mississippi was Biloxi, in 1699. That was apparently as important as Biloxi would ever be. Of late she had been surpassed in impor-

1

tance by such cities as Natchez and Vicksburg, because they were on the Mississippi River and Biloxi was on the Sound, and Jackson, which was the capital.

However, Clint found himself liking Biloxi as he walked its streets. It was a fairly large city, but its streets were not overcrowded. He found a small restaurant from which he could see the Mississippi Sound. He ordered a steak and it came cooked to his specifications. In addition, the beer was cold and the coffee hot and strong. Indeed, Biloxi was becoming very much to his liking.

After lunch he walked to a nearby saloon, exchanging greetings with both men and women on the street. He noticed that the women were extremely attractive. He wondered if this was why Moses had wanted him to meet him here, instead of in New Orleans, where their upriver trip was to start. Then again, New Orleans was notorious for its good food and fine women—or was it the other way around?

After one beer in the saloon he left and walked down to the docks. Here the pretty city of Biloxi was not all that attractive. Like any other city, its docks did not reflect its true personality. Rather, the personality of the docks was the same, no matter what city you were in, whether it was Biloxi, New York, or San Francisco.

J. P. Moses's *Biloxi Queen* was not hard to find. She was a fine-looking boat, painted bright colors and almost rivaling in sheer size Moses's *Dead Man's Chance*.

Clint approached the *Queen* and called out to one of its crew.

"What is it?" the man asked.

"Is Moses aboard?"

"He is."

"Would you tell him Clint Adams is here?"

The man waved and said, "I'll tell him."

While waiting, Clint thought about his friend. . . .

J. P. Moses had been born in Hard Time, Mississippi, along the banks of the Great River itself. Clint knew that Moses had hated the Mississippi ever since it took the lives of his mother and father. When he was placed in an orphanage, he discarded the name he was born with—Jean-Paul Bouchet—as if to punish his parents for dying. He took the name J. P. Moses for himself. He chose Moses because he had been the strongest man in the Bible. That was evidenced by the fact that he had been able to part the Red Sea. J. P. always thought that Moses probably could have parted the Mississippi, mud and all.

When he was fifteen he became enamored of an old gambler named Simon Chance. It was from Chance he learned all he could learn about cards, dice, all forms of gambling . . . and women. He hung on to his hatred of the Great River, though, because every time a boat left the dock Chance was on it.

When he was sixteen he left Mississippi to go west, vowing never to return. There he made his living with cards, dice, all forms of gambling, in all the tough gambling towns like Dodge City, Tombstone, and Abilene. When he was nineteen he was in Abilene, while Wild Bill Hickok was marshal. (Clint had been in Abilene during that time, but he and Moses did not meet then.) Five years later he was in Deadwood when Hickok was shot from behind and killed by the coward, Jack McCall.

J. P. learned how to use his fists and his guns in the West, but the greatest lesson he learned came to him while he was staring down at Hickok's body on the floor of Carl Mann's No. 10 saloon. He learned that it was foolish to hate something like a river, even the Mississippi. It was a waste of time, and time wasted was life wasted. Hickok's life was gone, but J. P. Moses's was still ahead of him.

That day he headed back to Hard Times to face down the Mississippi River, conquer it and make it *his* river . . . and he did just that. . . .

"What are you doing?" Moses shouted at Clint from aboard the *Biloxi Queen*. "Daydreaming? I said come on aboard!"

TWO

Moses gave Clint the tour of the *Biloxi Queen* and introduced him to some of the crew.

"I still have to hire some leadsmen," Moses said, "but I've got two fine pilots lined up, and good steersmen, good watchmen—"

"Aren't you planning on leaving tomorrow?"

"Yeah."

"And are you?"

"Sure," Moses said. "I can get some leadsmen along the way, maybe even in Fort Eads. I won't really need them until the start up the Mississippi anyway."

"If you pick one up in Fort Eads, or one of the Delta towns, he won't be the best, will he?"

"By whose standards?" Moses asked, laughing. "I've met some of the best river men in small river towns, Clint. Come on up to the bridge and I'll pour you a drink."

Clint knew Moses liked having a drink on the bridge, but once his boat was under way he never allowed liquor up there. If he found any of his men drunk he tossed them overboard, whether they were in a port or not.

As they entered the bridge Moses introduced Clint to a man named Mr. Bixby. Mr. Bixby was his main pilot. It had taken Clint some time to understand that each boat had at least two pilots *and* a captain.

"Mr. Bixby, this is my very good friend, Clint Adams," Moses said. "He is to have the run of the boat, understood?"

Bixby was in his fifties with a chin full of gray hair that extended up under his nose. It made him look as if he belonged in the Bible.

"Seems t'me that's somethin' you should be tellin' the captain, Mr. Moses."

"And I will be doing just that, Mr. Bixby. Would you happen to know where he is?"

"Not offhand."

Even Clint could tell that the man was lying.

"If he's drunk somewhere, Mr. Bixby, he'll go over the side."

"I'm sure he knows that, sir."

"He better."

Moses produced a bottle of whiskey from someplace, along with two shot glasses. He poured himself and Clint a glass each.

"Here's to the *Queen*," he said.

"I'll drink to that."

"How about something to eat?" Moses asked, stowing the bottle away.

Even though Clint had eaten something after he'd arrived, he found that he could still eat.

"Sounds good to me."

"Mr. Bixby?"

"Yes, sir?"

"Will you tell Captain Blowers—if you see him—that I will be wanting to talk to him when I return."

"Yes, sir."

"Carry on, then."

"Yes, sir."

"Carry on doing what?" Clint asked as they left the bridge.

"He's double-checking everything so we'll be ready to leave tomorrow."

Clint followed Moses off the boat and allowed the man to take the lead.

"There's a tavern nearby where we can eat and drink. The food's good, and the beer's cold."

"Good," Clint said. "We have some catching up to do. It's been a while since that riverboat race."

"Two years," Moses said.

"How's the *Dead Man's Chance* doing?"

"The *Chance* is fine."

"Not trading her in for the *Queen*, I hope?" Clint asked.

"Not a prayer," Moses said. "The *Dead Man's Chance* is my home."

"Then what are we doing in Biloxi?"

Moses slapped Clint on the back and said, "I'll tell you that over some beef stew and a beer."

THREE

"Okay," Clint said, when they had stew and beer in front of them, "why are we in Biloxi?"

"Because that's where the *Queen* was."

"And why did you want the *Queen*?"

Moses put down his fork and picked up his beer.

"I've wanted a second boat for a long time, Clint."

"For any particular reason?"

"To enhance my reputation."

"Jack," Clint said, "you're already the most famous gambler on the Mississippi. What more do you want?"

He was the only man Moses allowed to call him "Jack."

"I don't know, for sure," Moses said, "but I know I want more. I think having a second boat is the first step."

"And then what?" Clint asked. "A third?"

Moses shrugged.

"How did you decide on the *Queen*?"

"I heard about it from a steersman who worked on it. I looked into it and found out it was for sale."

"So you bought it?"

"Well . . . no."

"But you own it."

"Yes."

"And you didn't buy it?"

"Uh . . . no."

Clint sat back and eyed his friend for a few moments until he thought he had it figured out.

"You won it."

"Yes."

"How did you manage that?"

"I heard that the former captain was a gambler," Moses said.

"And you found out *where* he gambled."

"I heard he was going to be in a private game, and I got myself invited. That was when I sent my telegram to you."

"You invited me here before you knew you owned the boat?"

Moses nodded.

"Well," Clint said, "that's confidence for you."

"I didn't trick anyone, Clint, if that's what you're thinking," Moses said. "Everybody in that game was happy to have a shot at me."

"Didn't they think it was unusual for you to come this far from the Mississippi?"

"Nobody said anything."

"Jack, do you realize that this is the first time I can remember you being this far from the Mississippi in . . . well, years."

Moses chewed a mouthful of beef stew thoughtfully. Clint took the opportunity to shovel a few forkfuls into his mouth. It was excellent stew, even though the place itself looked as if it hadn't been cleaned since . . . well, since the last time J. P. Moses was this far from the Mississippi River.

"You know," Moses said finally, "I hadn't thought about that."

"How did you come to win the *Queen*?"

"The former captain, a fella named Masters, got into a

hand he shouldn't have, and had to put the boat up.''

"What did he have?"

"Four nines."

"And you?"

"A royal flush."

"Were you dealing?"

Moses grinned.

"No, I wasn't. You don't really think I'd cheat, do you?"

"No, I don't," Clint said. "I guess I was out of line."

"Well, Masters was, too. He accused me of cheating."

"And what happened?"

"I didn't kill him, if that's what you mean," Moses said. "I had him escorted from the game."

"When was that?"

"Last week," Moses said. "I've been outfitting her ever since then."

"And have you heard from Captain Masters since then?"

"No, not a word."

"Does that strike you as odd?"

"Now that you mention it," Moses said. "He was pretty upset."

"Think he'll offer to buy it back?"

"I doubt he'd have the money."

"Think he'll try to take it back?"

"That's a possibility."

Clint picked up his head.

"I didn't invite you for your gun, if that's what you're thinking," Moses said.

"I wasn't," Clint said. "You can use a gun pretty good yourself."

"Okay," Moses said, "now I was out of line."

"Forget it."

"Look," Moses said, "all I want to do is get the *Queen* to New Orleans. From there we're going to have a hell of a good time taking her to St. Paul and back to show her off."

"And after that?"

"I'll find somebody to run her, and I'll go back to the *Chance*. I'll make an appearance on the *Queen* from time to time."

"What do you mean by a good time?"

"I think you know what *I* mean by a good time, Clint," Moses said.

"Is Kelly Preston still dealing for you?"

Moses made a face.

"No, she left me soon after you left," Moses said. "You ruined her for the Mississippi, Clint."

"Where'd she go?"

"I don't know. She didn't stay in touch, but I've hired someone to deal on the *Queen*. Her name's Cinda Wolfe."

"Unusual name."

"She's an unusual woman," Moses said. "Smart, beautiful, and good at what she does."

"And she'll be on the *Queen*?"

"Yep," Moses said. "She'll be the only female dealer."

Clint knew that Moses did that on purpose. He only ever hired one woman at a time—and usually a beautiful one. It made her the center of attention for the male gamblers, who all wanted to gamble at her table. While they waited, though, they gambled at the other tables, and their concentration was not what it might have been—and it didn't get any better when they finally got to her table.

"Still up to your old tricks," Clint said.

"The old tricks are the best," Moses said. "What do you say, Clint? Are you in for the whole trip?"

"New Orleans to St. Paul, and back?"

"Yep."

"How long?"

"We're not going to look to set any records," Moses said. "We'll be stopping along the way to show her off. Baton Rouge, Natchez, Vicksburg, Memphis, Cairo, St. Louis, Alton—maybe even places like Cape Girardeau and St. Genevieve. Who knows?"

"You're asking me to put in a lot of time."

Moses laughed.

"I'm asking you to take a long vacation."

Clint thought about that and then said, "Yeah, you are at that."

FOUR

Moses offered Clint a room on the *Queen* so he wouldn't have to stay in a hotel overnight.

"I've already got the room, I might as well use it," Clint said. "Besides, I'd like to see Biloxi."

"It's not New Orleans, but it's got its charm," Moses admitted. "I'd show you around, but I've still got some hiring to do."

"And you want to see your captain."

Moses made a face and said, "I might be hiring a new captain, too."

"What about you?"

"What about me?"

"As captain, I mean."

"No," Moses said, shaking his head. "I know my limitations. I might be a fair pilot, but I'd never make a riverboat captain. They're a rare breed. Besides, the pay's not good enough."

Clint remembered Moses telling him one time that a riverboat captain made about two hundred and fifty dollars a month. He wondered if the amount had gone up since he was last on the Mississippi.

After they finished eating they left the tavern and stopped outside.

"Know your way back to your hotel?" Moses asked.

13

"I do."

"Then I'll see you on the *Queen* in the morning," Moses said.

"What time? First light?"

"God, no. We won't be leaving until about noon. You can come by anytime in the morning."

"All right."

"I can tell you where to go for some gambling, maybe some women, if you want."

"Thanks, but I think I'll just walk around a bit myself."

"Suit yourself," Moses said, clapping Clint on the shoulder. "It's good to see you again, friend."

"You, too, Jack."

"Off with you, now," Moses said. "I've got work to do."

Clint watched his friend walk away, then turned to go the other way. He stopped short, because something he had seen just seconds earlier, something that had not registered immediately, struck him. He turned back again, but Moses was out of sight. He could not force himself to walk away, though. He had a feeling of impending danger for his friend, and started after him.

He knew the way back to the docks and hurried along, convinced that Moses was in trouble. As he turned into an alley he saw that he was right.

Moses was in the middle of a fight with three men. He was giving as good as he got, but Clint knew that soon the numbers would tell on him. As he hurried to help Moses, Clint realized that he had seen the men follow Moses from the tavern; it simply had not registered with him immediately.

The three men Moses was tussling with were seamen by appearance. None of them wore gun belts, but they were all brandishing knives, as was Moses. A good seaman always carried a knife, and knew how to do many things with it—of which killing was just one.

Clint decided not to wade in but to use his gun to dissuade the men from continuing their attack. He drew and fired into the air twice, attracting their attention.

However, instead of breaking off the attack, one of the men shouted, "I'll take him," and pulled a gun from his belt. Clint shot him immediately. This caught the attention of the other two men, and Moses took the opportunity to bury his knife to the hilt in the stomach of one of them. The other man, seeing that he was now alone, ran off.

Clint reached Moses as he was bending over the man he'd stabbed.

"Who sent you?" Moses asked.

"I'll check the other one," Clint said.

Clint heard Moses repeat the question but knew his friend wouldn't be getting an answer anytime soon. The gray pallor of the stabbed man spoke volumes. He'd be dead in seconds, if he wasn't already.

Clint checked the man he'd shot and found that he was very dead. There was a Navy Colt on the ground next to him, and from the looks of it, it might have exploded in his hand if he'd had a chance to fire it.

"Dead?" Moses asked over his shoulder.

"Yes."

"Mine, too."

Clint straightened, replaced the spent shells in his gun with live ones, and holstered it.

"What made you come after me?" Moses asked. He'd removed his knife from the man's belly and put it back in its sheath.

"I caught a glimpse of them as they started after you," Clint said. "I figured you'd need help."

"You were right," Moses said. "I think they were going to kill me."

"Don't you have a gun?"

"It's on the *Queen*," Moses said. "I don't wear it all the time."

"Well," Clint said, "I think you better start. It looks like your friend Masters wants his boat back."

"You think he sent them?"

"Who else?"

"I do have other enemies."

Clint shook his head.

"Too much of a coincidence, Jack."

"I forgot how you hate coincidence."

"Maybe I better walk you back to the *Queen*."

"I don't think I need you to hold my hand, Clint," Moses said. "We took care of these two, and the third man is probably still running."

"Nevertheless," Clint said, "I think I'll take you up on your offer to sleep on the boat tonight."

"I won't argue with you, there," Moses said. "I'll feel a lot safer with you aboard."

FIVE

From the scene of the attack they went to Clint's hotel to collect his belongings, which included Duke. Moses assured Clint that there was a safe and comfortable place for the big gelding onboard the *Biloxi Queen*.

After the hotel they went to the police to tell them what had happened and where to find the two men. They also told them where they'd be.

Clint was unpacking his gear in his cabin when there was a knock on the door.

"Come in."

Moses opened the door and stepped in.

"The police are here," he said. "They want to talk to us."

"I'll be right with you."

"They sent someone named Lieutenant Clark."

"Know him?"

Moses shook his head.

"I haven't been to Biloxi often enough to know the local law."

"Where is he?"

"He's looking over the gambling setup, waiting for us in the main room."

"Good," Clint said, turning to face his friend. "I'd like to see that setup myself."

"Let's go, then."

•   •   •

The lieutenant was in his forties, a big man in many ways. He was tall, and wide, and he had huge hands. Clint knew that the man had to have his suits specially made for him. He was just too big to buy them any other way.

"Are you Mr. Adams?" he asked as Clint and Moses entered.

"That's right."

"Good to meet you."

Clint's hand virtually disappeared in the policeman's, but the man apparently had no need to prove his strength. He simply shook Clint's hand and released it.

"I've heard Mr. Moses's side of what happened this afternoon," Clark said. "I'd like to hear yours."

Clint told him, very concisely, what had happened after he and Moses left the tavern.

"You say you didn't notice them right away?" Clark asked.

"That's right," Clint said. "It took a few seconds to set in, but then I realized what was going on."

"How do you explain that, Mr. Adams?"

"Explain what, exactly?"

"That you knew what was going to happen?"

"Instinct, I guess," Clint said with a shrug.

Clark studied Clint for a few moments.

"I know your reputation, Mr. Adams."

"Do you?"

"Yes," Clark said, and then looked at Moses. "And I know yours. That's why I believe what you're telling me. Men like you probably need to have eyes in the back of your head all the time."

"It never hurts," Clint said, and Moses nodded.

"How much longer will you both be in Biloxi?" Clark asked.

"Just until tomorrow afternoon," Moses said.

"Well," the policeman said, "maybe you can stay out of trouble between now and then."

"We'll see what we can do, Lieutenant," Clint said.

"I'd appreciate it, gentlemen."

After Clark left, Moses looked at Clint and said, "Does he think we went looking for trouble?"

"It really doesn't matter who went looking, does it?" Clint asked. "All he knows is that we killed two men, and he doesn't want it to happen again."

"Well, it won't," Moses said, "unless somebody else wants to have a try at me."

"Maybe we should try to find Captain Masters," Clint said.

"I don't think we need to do that," Moses said. "Even if it was Masters who sent those men after me, we'll be heading out tomorrow afternoon."

Clint was thinking how much easier and shorter a trip it would be from Biloxi to New Orleans by land for Masters and anyone else he cared to send, but he decided not to argue with Moses at this point.

"Don't you have some more hiring to do?" he asked Moses.

"Yes, and I still have to talk to the captain—if he's sober."

"Why did you hire him if he's a drunk?"

"I didn't know he was," Moses said. "The man has a good reputation, and I hired him on the basis of that and one interview. It wasn't until after that I saw him drunk a couple of times."

"How many chances are you going to give him?"

"I'm going to let him take the boat to New Orleans. If we have a problem between here and there, then I'll make a change when we get there."

"Sounds fair. Well, let's get to it, then."

"Get to what?"

"You're going to be interviewing for leadsmen, or whatever, right?"

"And what are you going to do?"

"Me?" Clint said. "I'm going to be right there beside you, J. P. Remember, the lieutenant wants us to stay out of trouble. Maybe if we stick together we can do it. . . . maybe."

SIX

Clint went with Moses as he interviewed several men for two openings. Once the men were hired they were taken back to the *Biloxi Queen* and turned over to Mr. Bixby.

"Time for dinner," Moses announced when that was done.

It was almost seven p.m.

"Not at that tavern again."

"No, I think we'll eat onboard," Moses said. "I hired a chef yesterday, and I want to taste his food."

"Fine."

"We'll also be dining with some of the other people I hired," Moses said, "so why don't you go and dress for dinner."

"Women?" Clint asked.

"One or two."

"Going to sample their wares tonight, too, Jack?" Clint asked.

Moses cocked an eyebrow and said, "One never knows."

When Clint arrived in the main dining room, there were already three people sitting with Moses at a long captain's table that was fully set for dinner. One of them was a man

21

in his fifties who was working on a large glass of wine. Clint took this to be Captain Blowers.

There were two other men, sort of frowning across the table at Captain Blowers.

". . . don't have to worry about me," Blowers was saying. "When we're on the water and running I never touch a drop."

"I hope that's true, Captain," Moses replied.

Blowers looked at Moses with a scowl.

"Why would I lie, damn it?" he asked. "I don't want to lose my job any more than the next person does."

"I'm glad to hear it, Captain . . . ah," Moses said, breaking off when he saw Clint, "here's someone I want you all to meet."

Clint approached the table, and Moses made introductions.

"Clint Adams, this is our captain, Adam Blowers."

In greeting, Blowers raised his wineglass while still seated.

"And these are our two pilots, Sam Castle and Ben Haggerty."

Clint shook hands with the two men, who stood during the introductions. Castle was in his thirties and was probably very experienced, while Haggerty looked to be in his early twenties. Clint wondered how much experience he had.

"Well, Clint, have a seat," Moses said. "As usual, the ladies are fashionably late."

"Ladies?" Clint asked.

"Yes, two of them, both young, both pretty, gentlemen, so I'll remind you about my rule of no fraternizing among the employees, understood?"

"Yes, sir," Haggerty said, but he seemed the only one

of the three men at the table who took the comment seriously.

"One of the ladies is my blackjack dealer," Moses said. He looked across the table at Clint. "We discussed her earlier today. Her name is Cinda Wolfe."

"I remember," Clint said. "Who is the other one?"

"Ah, here they are now," Moses said. He stood, and the others followed suit, even Captain Blowers, although he did hang on to his drink glass.

Clint turned and watched the two women enter the room. They were certainly a contrast to each other.

The first woman had red hair, the second black. The first was slight, probably not even five feet tall, while the second was certainly five nine, possibly more. Both, however, possessed eye-catching bodies, which they showed off in low-cut gowns. The redhead had small, perfect-looking breasts, while the dark-haired woman had large, round, firm breasts. The only thing the two women had in common was pale skin. Obviously, they both spent most of their time indoors.

"Gentlemen, this is Miss Cinda Wolfe...." The redhead smiled at them all. "And this is Miss Laura Giles." The dark-haired woman smiled and inclined her head.

"Please, ladies, be seated and we'll start dinner. Cinda, you there, and Laura, there."

Moses directed the ladies where to sit, and Clint found himself with a woman on either side of him. He looked down at Moses and silently thanked him.

As if they'd been watching and waiting, two servers entered the room, both men in their fifties wearing white jackets and bow ties. They were carrying soup tureens, and began ladling soup into the bowls on the table.

"This smells wonderful," Cinda Wolfe said.

"I think we should establish that we're all on a first name basis here," Moses said.

Clint remembered the first names of all the people at the table. He wondered how many of the others could, as well.

"Mr. Moses tells me you're going to be the blackjack dealer," Clint said to Cinda.

"That's right. Do you play?"

"I've been known to, but poker is more my game."

"Clint is an excellent poker player," Moses said.

"Not in Moses's class," Clint said.

"Nonsense," Moses said. "He's played with the best, and that includes Luke Short and Bat Masterson."

"Do you know Bat Masterson?" Laura Giles asked.

"Yes," Clint said, "he's a good friend of mine."

"I'd love to meet him someday," she said. "I've heard so much about him."

Clint found himself looking down her dress at her impressive cleavage, and pulled his eyes away before she noticed—if she hadn't already. What the hell, she was probably used to it, and didn't she wear a low-cut gown? He looked again, and she smiled at him.

He turned to look at Cinda, and while her cleavage was almost as impressive—on a smaller scale, of course—what caught his eye was her face. Laura was pretty, but Cinda was a beauty in every sense of the word. She had green eyes shaped like a cat's, and a wide mouth. Laura's eyes were brown, more rounded, and her lips were full, her mouth not as wide. It was difficult to assess her age, and it probably always would be. She'd always have a very young appearance, like a big little girl—but with a woman's body . . . definitely!

Clint noticed the other men at the table were also eyeing the women, and looking at him with envy for his position at the table—but then he wasn't a member of the crew, so there was nothing to keep *him* from fraternizing with either of the ladies.

It occurred to him that he still didn't know what Laura's job was going to be.

"Are you a dealer, like Cinda?" he asked. The others were talking to each other, so no one could hear their conversation.

"Oh, no," she said, "I have another job entirely."

"And what would that be?"

"I'm in charge of the girls."

Clint frowned.

"What girls?"

"Didn't Mr. Moses tell you?"

"Tell me what?"

"Well," she said, "I'm a madam."

SEVEN

"A floating whorehouse?" Clint asked Moses later. "I'm surprised at you, Jack."

"Seems to me I heard someplace that you owned a whorehouse once."

"I didn't own it, exactly," Clint said. "I won it."

"So?"

"I got rid of it," Clint said. "I didn't want to run a whorehouse."

They were still in the dining room, while the others had all finished and left. The captain had taken a bottle of wine with him to his room. Before leaving, Laura had made it clear to Clint that she wouldn't mind if he came to her room later . . . just so they could finish talking.

"I don't want to run one, either."

"Then why are you?"

"I'm not," Moses argued. "It's just another service we'll be offering on the *Queen*."

"You never did this on the *Chance*."

"I know," Moses said, "that's why I decided to experiment with it."

"Laura seems a little young to be a madam."

"She's thirty," Moses said, "although I know she looks younger. She's got the proper experience, though."

"As a whore?"

"Well, yes, but she's also run a few houses before. She'll do a good job looking after the girls."

"And where *are* the girls?" Clint asked. "Are they on-board?"

"No," Moses said, "they'll come onboard in New Orleans."

"And what about this rule about not fraternizing?" Clint asked. "How are you going to enforce that with so many women aboard?"

"Hey, I don't mind if the men sample the merchandise from time to time, as long as it doesn't interfere with the paying customers."

"And what about you?"

"What about me?"

"Have you sampled the merchandise yet?"

"You mean Cinda and Laura? No. If you're wondering whether I will or not, probably not, but who knows? I'll have to see what the other girls look like. I'm not above taking a whore to bed now and then."

Clint wasn't, either, he just wasn't about to pay for the privilege.

"Jack," Clint said, "nobody's ever put a floating whore-house on the Mississippi before. How do you think people are going to react?"

"Well," Moses said, pouring them each some more wine, "the men will love it, and the women will hate it— and it's not a floating whorehouse. The girls will just be one service we'll provide. The primary service will still be the gambling."

"Gambling and women," Clint said, shaking his head. "That combination has been the downfall of a lot of men."

"Well," Moses said, raising his glass, "here's to them losing their money to me on the way down."

EIGHT

Most of Clint's conversation at the dinner table had been with Laura Giles. That's why he was surprised when he got to his cabin to find Cinda Wolfe in his bed—naked.

"Surprised?" she asked, keeping herself covered with the sheet. The way it molded itself to her body, though, her condition beneath it was obvious.

"Very."

"Pleasantly?"

"Oh," he said, "very."

"Want me to leave?"

"I guess that depends on what you want."

She tossed the sheet away and said, "What do you think I want?"

He smiled and said, "Don't leave, then."

He approached the bed and sat next to her, staring down at her face, and then her nude body. Her breasts were small and round, with pink nipples that were already hard. The patch of hair between her perfect little thighs was a rusty color, just a bit darker than the hair on her head. He didn't know how long she had been waiting, but he could smell her readiness. She gave off the delightful odor of sex, mixed with her own smell, and the scent of whatever perfume she was wearing. The combination was quite heady.

"I bet you thought you'd find Laura here," she said, putting her hand on his chest.

"The thought had crossed my mind."

"Well, she wanted to come," Cinda said, beginning to unbutton his shirt, "but I told her to stay away from you. I told her you were mine."

"And when did you decide that?"

She had his shirt open and slid her hand inside. Her palm was warm on his chest.

"As soon as I saw you."

She slid the shirt off his shoulders and dropped it on the floor.

"Take off the rest of your clothes," she said. "I want to watch."

Clint understood this request because he himself enjoyed watching women dress and undress. He stood up and removed his boots and the remainder of his clothes.

"I knew it," she said, looking at his erect penis.

"Knew what?"

"Knew you'd be beautiful," she said, then reached out and touched him and added, "there."

Her touch was featherlight and it made him jump.

"Lie back," he said.

"Why?"

"I want to get to know you."

"How?"

He smiled and said, "With my mouth."

"Oooh . . ." she said, and did as she was told.

Clint stood beside the bed a moment, looking at her, trying to decide where to start. He had to admit that his favorite part of a naked woman was her breasts, and Cinda certainly had beautiful ones. Abruptly, however, he decided to start at her feet and work his way up. She was beautiful, and she looked delicious, as well. He wanted to examine every part of her, every line, fold, and orifice of her with his mouth and tongue. By the time he was finished he hoped to have her so excited she wouldn't be able to contain herself.

"I'm going to devour you," he said.

She extended her arms up over her head, stretching until her breasts were taut, and said, "I knew you'd be an interesting lover."

He spent the better part of an hour on her, pushing her hands away any time she reached for him. He kissed her feet, sucking her toes until she squealed. They were delicate, pretty feet, and he suddenly found himself fascinated by them. It was with an effort that he pulled himself away from them, kissed her ankles, and then continued upward. The flesh of her thighs was incredibly smooth and warm, and he closed his eyes and rubbed his lips over them.

"God . . ." she said once, and then fell silent again.

He kissed her knees, and then behind her knees, lifting her legs straight up so he could get to that area. When her legs were in the air he decided to keep them there. He slid his hand down one of her thighs until he pressed his palm against her rusty pubic hair. Her pubis was hot and wet, and he slid one finger over the folds of her skin, making her catch her breath and squeeze her eyes shut. He found her clit with his thumb and just brushed against it lightly.

"Oh, God—" she said, and then bit her lip.

He stopped teasing her and eased her legs back down to the bed. He pressed his mouth to her belly, kissing her, and then continued up. He touched his tongue to her navel, which was deep, then kissed her ribs lightly, causing her to laugh softly.

"That tickles . . ." she complained, but she did not try to stop him.

Finally, he reached her breasts, and they were so adorable that he decided to spend a lot of time on them.

He touched his tongue to each nipple, licking it lightly, then swirling it around, wetting her, then sucking her. She moaned and reached for his head, but he pushed her hands away.

"I can't do this—" she started, but he cut her off.

"No hands," he said, "not until I say so."

Reluctantly she put her hands back down on the bed, but took great handfuls of the sheet.

He kissed the upper slopes of her breasts, ran his tongue down between them, and then licked the smooth, warm skin of the undersides. She was smaller than he would have preferred had he had a choice, possibly one of the smallest women he'd ever been with, but there was no denying her beauty or her appeal—or the taste of her!

By now her whole body was taut. He abandoned her breasts to kiss her shoulders and her neck. When he reached her mouth she opened it and almost devoured his tongue. When she reached up to put her arms around him this time he didn't stop her.

"Oh, God," she said, against his mouth, "I want you, I want you in me!"

And he wanted it as much as she did. His penis was throbbing as he straddled her and touched the head to her pubis. She was so wet that he slid in as if he'd been greased. She gasped, wrapped her arms and legs around him, and fastened her mouth to his again. She sucked on his tongue as he drove himself into her, deeper and deeper. She might have been small, but he was surprised by how strong she was.

He slid his hands down beneath her to cup her buttocks, and she was so wet that she had soaked the sheet beneath them. He didn't care, though. In fact, it made him more excited. He squeezed her buttocks, pulling her to him as he drove into her. Her face was pressed against his shoulder, and he could hear her breathing heavily, grunting as they came together.

"Oh . . . oh . . . oh, God . . ." she said, and then she was bucking beneath him as spasms of pleasure shook her body, and then he groaned aloud as he emptied into her. . . .

NINE

Clint sat up in bed abruptly.

"What is it?" Cinda asked from beside him.

They had fallen asleep soon after their lovemaking, without even having a chance to talk. They still had not learned much about each other beyond what they might have heard at the dinner table.

"What is it?" she asked again.

"I don't know," he said, and he didn't. "Something woke me up."

"What?"

"I don't know," he repeated, "but I have to go and check it out."

He got up and quickly pulled on his trousers, then took his gun from his holster.

"Stay here," he said.

"Don't worry," she said, pulling the sheet over her, "I will."

As he started for the door she called out, "Be careful."

"Don't worry," he said, before leaving, "I will."

Outside on deck it was dark. The moon was just a sliver in the sky. Clint paused and waited for his eyes to adjust, then continued. The night air gave him gooseflesh on his naked torso. He heard something behind him and whirled

33

around. He found himself pointing his gun at J. P. Moses, who was in turn pointing *his* gun at him.

"Don't sneak up on me like that!" Clint snapped.

"I couldn't sneak up on you if I tried," Moses replied. "Why are you out here?"

"I don't know," Clint said. "Something woke me up. What about you?"

"Same thing. What do you suppose it was?"

"I don't know, but you go that way, and I'll go this way, and maybe we'll find out."

"All right," Moses said, "but sing out when you see or hear something."

"Right."

"And don't shoot me!"

"I'll keep that in mind."

Moses turned and they went in opposite directions.

Clint kept moving until he reached the gangplank. It would have been very easy for someone to board the boat while they were all asleep, since the gangplank was still down. He stared down at the dock but couldn't see anybody there. If someone was on the boat, they weren't there for any good purpose. All he could think was that someone— Captain Masters? friends of the men they'd killed?—might have boarded the boat for the purpose of revenge.

He heard something behind him and turned quickly. He hoped it wasn't Moses or one of his men because this time he wasn't taking any chances. He fired, and his bullet struck a silhouette, which fell to the deck. He approached, knowing that if he had shot J. P. Moses his friend would never forgive him.

He reached the fallen figure and turned it over. It wasn't Moses, and it wasn't anybody he knew. Whoever it was, he was wounded but alive. The man's gun was on the deck, and Clint picked it up and tossed it overboard. He heard it hit the water with a splash.

"Who sent you?" he demanded.

The man remained silent, compressing his lips in pain.

"You need a doctor, friend," Clint said. "If you want one you better answer my questions. How many of you came aboard?"

The man resisted a moment longer, then said, "Three."

"And who sent you?"

"Don't know," the man said. "We was hired . . . by Dillon . . ."

"Who's Dillon?"

"He's . . . on the boat, too. . . ."

"What were you hired to do?"

"Mess up the boat."

"And kill somebody?"

"Mister . . . I'm hurt bad . . . I can feel it . . . I'm burnin' up . . ."

"Too bad," Clint said. "Stay here and don't try to move. If you're still alive by the time I find your friends I'll get you a doctor."

Clint stood up.

"Hey, you can't—"

"You want to get tossed in the water now?" Clint asked.

The man fell silent.

Just then Clint heard a shot and ran toward it.

When he reached the other side of the boat, he found Moses crouching over a body.

"Is he dead?" Clint asked.

"You bet," Moses said. "I wasn't taking any chances. You get one?"

"Yeah," Clint said. "He's not dead, but he will be soon."

"Did he talk?"

Clint nodded.

"There's one more onboard somewhere."

"Who sent them?"

"They're just hired help," Clint said. "One of them is named Dillon. He hired the other two."

"And who hired him?"

"We can ask him when we find him," Clint said, then looked down at the dead man and added, "unless that's him."

"Let's look around and find out," Moses said, "and let's do it together, so we don't shoot each other this time."

"That's fine by me."

They heard running footsteps just then and took off in that direction. They heard someone going down the gangplank.

"Damn," Moses shouted, "he's getting away. . . ."

They charged down the gangplank after him, but by the time they reached the dock the man was gone.

"No point in charging around in the dark, Jack," Clint said. "Let's go back onboard."

"Maybe we can still get something out of the one you shot."

They went back onboard the *Biloxi Queen*, but by the time they reached the man Clint had shot, he was dead.

"What do we do with them?" Clint said.

"Throw them overboard?" Moses asked.

They stared at each other.

"If we call the police in the morning, that lieutenant is going to give us a hell of a time," Clint said.

"We probably won't be able to get under way when we want to."

Clint nodded.

"And why give the poor man any more aggravation?"

"You have a point."

They stared at each other a little bit longer.

"If we're going to do it," Clint finally said, "let's do it before I freeze to death."

TEN

They decided it would be better to weight down the bodies so that if they did somehow come back to the surface it would be after they were gone.

They dropped the bodies over the side, hoping no one would ask about the splashes. There was no one on the docks to hear their shots, or to see what they were doing.

"Anybody in your cabin?" Moses asked when they were done.

"Uh, yeah. You?"

"Uh-huh."

"What are you going to tell her?"

"As little as possible."

"That's a good idea."

"Prowlers," Moses said, "and we chased them away."

"We fired warning shots," Clint said.

"And they jumped overboard."

"Makes sense to me."

Moses nodded, and they both went back inside.

"What happened?" Cinda asked as Clint reentered the cabin.

"There were some prowlers onboard."

"I heard shots," she said. "Two shots."

"Moses and I chased them away," Clint said, slipping out of his pants and sitting on the bed.

"Are you all right?" she asked, touching him.

"Oh, sure," Clint said.

"They didn't shoot at you?"

"No," he said. "We fired over their heads and they jumped overboard."

"Well, that's good," she said. "I was worried."

"Nothing to worry about."

She touched his back and said, "Come to bed. You're cold."

He slid into bed with her, and she wrapped her warmth around him.

When Moses entered his cabin, Laura Giles looked at him from the bed.

"Are you all right?"

"Fine," he said, and gave her the same story Clint had given to Cinda.

Laura sat up and the sheet fell away from her. Moses stared with great pleasure at her big, firm breasts. She smiled, realizing what he was doing, and then extended her arms to him.

"Come to bed," she said, "I'll warm you."

"Yes," he said, joining her in bed, enjoying the feel of her hot flesh against his, "you certainly will."

ELEVEN

When Clint woke the next morning Cinda was lying with her back to him, her little butt pressed into his crotch. It didn't take long before his erect penis pressing against her woke her up. Without turning around she spread her legs. He reached around to touch her, rub her until she was wet. He slid his penis between her thighs and into her, and she moaned and pressed her face into the pillow.

They moved together that way for a while, making smacking noises as she became wetter, and then she reached down and pushed him away, then grabbed his penis and pulled it toward her butt. He knew what she wanted. He placed the wet head of his penis, slick with her juices, against her anus and pressed gently. The spongy head slid in first, and he was gentle with her until he was all the way inside of her. He reached around and slid his hand between her legs and began to stroke her as he moved in and out of her. She caught her breath, then began to moan into the pillow. He slid his other arm under her so he could stroke one of her breasts at the same time, thus stimulating her in three places at once.

He could feel her whole body shudder as he continued to work on her. His own pleasure was rising, as well, especially when she clenched her buttocks, closing tightly around him.

They kept moving together, although many of her moves were involuntary. She was feeling so many sensations at one time that she didn't have full control of her body. Finally, Clint roared and exploded inside of her, grunting as he continued to move. She whimpered and he felt her body begin to jerk uncontrollably, and he knew that a rarity had occurred. They had achieved their pleasure together.

As he slid from her he was so sensitive and she was so tight that he cried out again. He moved away from her, and she rolled up into a tight ball, her body still jerking spasmodically.

"Are you all right?" he asked.

"Oooh," she moaned, "God, I never . . . never felt anything like that before."

He touched her and her body was so sensitive she actually flinched. If her whole body felt the way his penis felt, he didn't blame her.

"Cinda?"

"I'll be fine," she said, stretching her legs out. "I'm just so . . . my heart's pounding . . . but I'll be fine."

Clint settled down on his back and waited for his own heart to stop pounding.

It was some time later before they both managed to sit up and talk about it.

"That's never happened to me before," she said.

"Exactly what happened?"

"It was just so . . . I mean, you were *touching* me in so many places at once . . ."

"Have you ever done it that way before?"

"You mean from behind? Well, yes, but . . . never with this result. I mean . . . I've never been with someone that way when it didn't . . . didn't hurt."

"Then why do it?"

"Well," she said, looking away, "there were times when I didn't have much of a choice."

"So why with me?"

Now she looked at him.

"I could tell you'd be different, gentle, and you were. It was . . . unbelievable."

"Yes," he said, "it was."

"For you, too?"

"Yes."

She smiled.

"I'm glad."

He didn't know what to say after that.

"Oh, don't look so worried," she said, laughing, "it doesn't mean I'm in love or anything."

"No?"

"No," she said, "but it does mean I hope you'll be around for a while. I mean, I'd like to find out if this was a . . . a fluke, or if it could happen again."

"Maybe it could," he said. "I guess we'll see."

"Right now," she said, "I'm so hungry I could eat a horse."

"Will there be breakfast in the dining room?" he asked, since she worked for Moses.

"Yes," she said, "Mr. Moses said we'd always be able to eat onboard, if we wanted to."

"Well," he said, "I guess we want to. We better get dressed."

"I wonder," she said, "if I can stand up."

Moses rolled away from Laura, totally spent.

"Wow," she said.

"I know."

"That was . . ."

"I know."

She rolled onto her back, her big breasts flattening against her chest. He smiled, leaned over and kissed each nipple.

"Better get dressed," he said. "We'll want to get an early breakfast so I can help get the *Queen* ready to go."

She stretched her body, almost enticing him to grab her again.

He tossed the sheet over her and said, "That's not fair. I'm going back to my cabin to get dressed. I'll see you at breakfast."

After he left she lay there a few moments, wondering if this was going to be a regular thing with him, or if it would happen every once in a while, or never again.

She hoped it wasn't the last one. J. P. Moses was all man, and he fit her just fine.

She thought that working for him might just be the best move she'd ever made.

TWELVE

Clint and Moses were the first ones down to breakfast. Both Cinda and Laura decided they needed a bath before they could get dressed. That suited both men. It gave them a chance to talk before anyone else appeared.

"Do you have any second thoughts about what we did?" Moses asked Clint over coffee.

"No," Clint said. "We can't afford second thoughts if you want to get under way today, Jack."

"I know," Moses said. "So did you get along well with Cinda?"

"What about you and Laura?"

Since they were the only two women onboard at the moment it wasn't hard to figure who was with who.

"We got along fine."

"Are you going to keep it going?"

"I don't know," Moses said. "I guess it depends on the other girls. There might be one I like better. Of course, eventually I'll be back on the *Chance* and she'll still be here on the *Queen.*"

"Then the answer's no."

Moses made a face.

"Can't stay with the same woman too long, Clint. It gets stale."

Clint didn't respond.

"What about you and Cinda? Gonna keep that going?"

"Maybe," Clint said, "for a while. But like you said, eventually she'll be here on the *Queen* and I'll be gone."

"Hey," Moses said, "as long as she knows that, where's the harm?"

"No harm," Clint said.

At that point both Cinda and Laura entered, and they were talking and laughing. Clint wondered if they had compared notes. He noticed Moses watching them, probably thinking the same thing.

There wasn't much time to talk to the women, though, as the two pilots entered almost right behind them. They all sat down and breakfast was served.

They were finishing up breakfast when Mr. Bixby entered.

"You're late, Mr. Bixby," Moses said, "but you can still eat."

"That's fine," Bixby said, "but there's a fella up on deck wants to see you."

"Oh? Who is he?"

"Says his name is Masters," Bixby said, "says he's the former captain of this boat."

Clint and Moses exchanged a glance, and Moses stood up.

"I'll go with you," Clint said, and followed Moses to the door.

On deck was a tall, grizzled man in his late fifties. There wasn't an ounce of fat on him, and Clint thought he looked like a good wind would blow him over—but he doubted that was the case.

"What do you want, Masters?" Moses demanded.

Masters squinted at Moses, closing one eye against the morning sun's glare.

"Wanted to give you one last chance to do right, Moses," the man said.

"How's that?"

"Gimme back my boat."

"You saying you want to buy it back?"

"Don't have to," Masters said. "It's mine."

"Not anymore," Moses said. "You lost it, and now it belongs to me."

"You cheated."

"I didn't," Moses said. "You're just a bad card player, Masters. You never should have bet it."

Masters glared at J. P. Moses for a few seconds, then looked at Clint.

"Who's this, your hired gunny?"

"Do I need a hired gun?" Moses asked. "Is that what you're telling me, Masters? You gonna send somebody after me? Or have you done that already?"

"You're gonna have trouble all right, Moses," Masters said. "Got to, because this boat ain't rightly yours."

"I think the police might be interested in talking to you, Mr. Masters," Clint said.

"*Captain* Masters," the man said, straightening his spine.

"Sorry," Clint said. "Captain Masters."

"Why would the law want to talk to me?"

"Seems a couple of men tried to kill Mr. Moses yesterday," Clint said. "We were wondering if they might have been friends of yours."

Masters didn't answer right away, then said, "Who knows? They might have, and then again, they might not. Then again, I don't know who you're talkin' 'bout, do I?"

"Don't you?" Clint asked.

Masters ignored Clint and looked at Moses.

"I gave you another chance, Moses," he said. "Now whatever happens is on your head."

He turned and walked to the gangplank, then spun around.

"This boat's bad luck for all but the rightful owner," he said. "You're gonna find that out."

"Get off my boat, Masters."

Masters surprised Clint by grinning, because he didn't see what the man had to smile about.

"You'll see," Masters said, and then he started down the gangplank, cackling like a fool or a madman.

"Think he sent those men last night?" Clint asked.

"I think he sent them all," Moses said. "Probably should've killed the old fool right here and now and been done with it."

They watched as Masters made his way to one end of the dock, and then Clint noticed a man approaching the boat from the other end.

"Uh-oh," he said.

"What?"

Clint jerked his head in the direction of the second man.

"Lieutenant Clark," Moses said. "Now what's he want?"

"I guess we're going to find out."

"Think he heard about last night?"

"How could he have?"

Moses shrugged.

"An anonymous tip."

"There aren't any bodies for him to find, unless he wants to drag the bottom of the Sound," Clint said. "Why don't we just wait and see what he has to say."

"I've got to get my boat ready to go," Moses said. "Why don't you talk to him, and if he wants to see me, come and get me."

"Okay," Clint said, "I'll take care of it, if I can."

"Thanks."

Moses turned and left, and Clint moved toward the gangplank to intercept the lieutenant.

THIRTEEN

"Good morning, Mr. Adams," the lieutenant said, ascending the gangplank.

"Lieutenant," Clint said. "What brings you here this morning?"

"Curiosity, I guess," the man said. He stopped, unable to board because Clint was blocking his way. "May I come aboard?"

"Oh, of course," Clint said, moving out of the way. "Pardon me."

The policeman came aboard and faced Clint.

"Have you spent much time on a riverboat, Mr. Adams?" he asked.

"Not much," Clint said, "but from time to time."

"Are you friends with Mr. Moses?"

"Yes."

"Long time?"

"Yes," Clint said. "Just what is it you're curious about, Lieutenant?"

"You, I guess," Clark said. "I know both of you by reputation, but Moses's appearance in Biloxi is not surprising."

"And mine is?"

"Frankly, yes."

"So you're curious why I'm in your city?"

"Yes."

"Well, I won't be for long," Clint said. "We leave today, so you don't have any worries."

The lieutenant nodded, then looked around the boat. He saw a couple of crewmen working, one with a mop, then looked back at Clint.

"I don't see Mr. Moses around."

"He's making preparations to leave," Clint said. "You *do* want us to leave, don't you?"

"Oh, yes," Clark said, "I do want you to leave, Mr. Adams. Please don't take it personally."

"I don't."

"You see, men like yourselves attract trouble, and I hate trouble."

"Dealing with trouble is your job, isn't it, Lieutenant?" Clint asked. "Maybe we're just supplying you with your job."

"I wouldn't mind a bit if my job was boring, Mr. Adams."

Clint looked past the policeman and saw with a start that he hoped he hid well that there was blood on the deck, blood from the man he'd shot. He thought that if the lieutenant turned around he'd surely see it.

"Is that all, Lieutenant?" he asked. "Or is there something else?"

"Well, I thought I might take a turn around the boat for you, you know, just to make sure there's no trouble brewing."

"I don't think that's necessary, Lieutenant," Clint said.

"Why not?"

"Mr. Moses is capable of handling his own affairs on the boat. It strikes me that your job is handling things *off* the boat."

Clark studied Clint for a few moments and then said, "You might be right about that."

Clark walked to the gangplank and turned, and Clint stood so he'd be between the man and the bloodstains.

"If you're still here tonight, Mr. Adams," he said, "I don't think I'd like it very much."

"I'll tell you what, Lieutenant," Clint said. "Neither would I."

Clark turned and went down the gangplank. Clint watched him until he was out of sight, then he turned to the deckhand with the mop.

"Swab that up, will you?" he said, pointing to the blood.

The deckhand, knowing that Clint was a friend of his boss, said, "Sure thing."

As Clint walked away he heard the man wonder aloud, "Is that blood?"

FOURTEEN

Clint found Moses and told him about his conversation with Lieutenant Clark. He also suggested that Moses have a talk with the deckhand who had swabbed up the blood about what he did or didn't see. Moses told him not to worry, his people were loyal. If he was ever asked, the deckhand would not tell anyone that he saw something that might have been blood.

For the rest of the morning Clint tried to stay out of the way of the crew, who were readying the boat to depart. He found himself in the dining room with Cinda and Laura, who were also staying out of the way.

"I guess we're the only nonessential people," Clint said.

"Speak for yourself," Laura said, and then added, "although from what I hear you're pretty damned essential."

"Laura!" Cinda said, slapping the larger woman on the arm.

Clint didn't know if Cinda and Laura had known each other before coming aboard, but whether they had or not they seemed to be pretty friendly now.

"I'm going to my room," Laura said, then asked, "or is it a cabin?"

"It's a cabin," Clint said.

"Well, whatever it is, it's got a pretty comfortable bed in it," Laura said, giving Clint a sly glance. Was she inviting him to join her? "Since I'm nonessential, I might as well get some rest. I didn't actually sleep all that well last night. I guess I'll just leave you two alone to . . . talk."

She gave both Clint and Cinda a last leering glance and then left them alone, as promised.

"She's bad," Cinda said, shaking her head.

Clint took the opportunity to ask her the question he'd been thinking about.

"Have you two been friends long?"

"About two days," Cinda said, laughing, "but we're already friends. I think she's wonderful."

"But bad."

"Oh, yes," she said, "very bad."

He moved closer to her, and they stood by the empty table.

"You told her about us, didn't you?"

"Yes, I did," Cinda admitted. "Girl talk. I hope you're not embarrassed?"

"No."

"Because if you are," she went on, "she told me everything, too. Would you like to know how Mr. Moses likes to—"

"No," he said, cutting her off hastily, "I would not care to know that, thank you."

Cinda laughed.

"Men don't talk to each other about things like that, do they?"

"I don't know about most men," he said, "but this man doesn't."

"You mean you didn't tell Mr. Moses what I like, or what I don't like," she asked, "or tell him what we did together?"

"No."

"Why not?"

"First of all," Clint said, "that's our business, and second of all, you work for the man. Why would I take a chance of embarrassing you?"

She stared at him for a few moments, then said, "You're really pretty special, aren't you?"

Slightly embarrassed, he said, "That's not for me to say."

"Well, I'm saying it." She got up on her toes and kissed him shortly on the mouth. "You are."

"Well . . . thanks."

"Well, now I've embarrassed you, haven't I?"

"A little," Clint said.

Then she gave him the same kind of look Laura had given him before leaving.

"I have a suggestion."

"What is it?"

"Since we're both nonessential people, as far as the crew is concerned, we could sort of . . . disappear. . . . " she said, leaving the rest to his imagination.

He had a good imagination, and they went to his cabin to explore it.

They were tightly locked together, Clint buried deep inside her, when the boat lurched and began moving away from the dock, surprising both of them.

"God!" she said in his ear, her voice a raspy whisper because she'd been breathing so hard. "Was that us, or is the boat leaving the dock?"

"The boat's leaving," he assured her, looking down at her lovely face.

"Mmmm," she said, wrapping her legs around him and

tightening her insides, ''I thought maybe we had moved the earth.''

''Well, let's just figure we could have, if we weren't on the water.''

She kissed him, pushing her tongue past his lips, and he began to move again, sliding his hands beneath her to cup her buttocks and bring her to him as he thrust at her again and again, this time *trying* to move the earth. . . .

FIFTEEN

"I had the feeling Laura was inviting me to her cabin before," Clint said, as they lay side by side later.

"She was flirting, no doubt about it," Cinda said, "and if you went to her cabin she'd probably let you in—in fact, if we both went to her cabin I think she'd let us in—but I think she was pretty happy with Mr. Moses last night."

"Really?"

"Mmm."

"And were you pretty happy last night?"

She smiled and said, " 'Pretty happy' doesn't begin to describe it."

"That's good," Clint said.

"You made sure of that."

"I did?"

"You know you did," she said, snuggling up to him. "I've never been with a man who was so concerned about my feelings. Do you treat all your women like that?"

"Oh, yes," he said, "every one of them."

"And how many have there been?"

"Dozens," he said, "hundreds . . . a whole army."

"I'll bet that's the truth, too."

He didn't say anything.

"Were you serious?" he asked then.

"About what?"

"Laura," he said. "Do you really think she'd let us both—"

She cut him off with an elbow to the ribs.

J. P. Moses watched as Captain Blowers took the *Biloxi Queen* out into the Mississippi Sound. The man seemed very competent at the moment—and very sober, but it remained to be seen how he would handle the boat on the Mississippi, where the bottom could come up and smack you in the face at any time.

Moses looked at Mr. Bixby and saw that he, too, was watching Blowers. Moses had worked with Bixby before and trusted his judgment. He gave a jerk of his head for Bixby to follow him out.

"What do you think?" Moses asked.

"He seems to know what he's doin' on the Sound, but that don't mean he knows the Mississippi. We'll have to wait and see."

"That's how I feel," Moses said. "All right, carry on. Keep an eye on him for me."

"Yes, sir."

Bixby went back onto the bridge while Moses went downstairs. Just on a hunch he stopped by Laura's cabin and knocked on the door.

"Who is it?"

"It's J. P. Moses."

"Well, come in."

Moses opened the door and entered. Laura was in bed with the sheet covering her. She was naked beneath it. He could see the outline of her big breasts and nipples.

"I was taking a nap," she said.

"I didn't mean to wake you."

"That's all right," she said, "that is, depending on what you had in mind."

"I think you know what I had in mind, Laura."

"Well," she said, "I can't very well refuse my boss, can I?"

"Actually," he said, "you can. That's one of the things I came down to tell you. In spite of what happened last night I wanted you to know that you're under no obligation to sleep with me just because I'm your boss."

She stared at him for a few moments, digesting what he was telling her. It wasn't that she didn't understand the words, it's just that no man had ever spoken them to her before.

"Why that's . . . that's very decent of you, Mr. Moses. Thank you."

"Sure," he said. "I'll just . . ." He reached for the door.

"But . . ." she said, getting his attention, "what if I just want to? Would that be all right?"

"Why, Miss Giles," Moses said, turning back to her, "that would be just fine."

"Oh," she said, discarding the sheet with one sweep of her arm, "I think it'll be more than just fine, don't you?"

SIXTEEN

Captain Blowers successfully took the boat between Horn Island and Ship Island and passed the Chandeleur Islands. From there they went by Grand Gosier Island, Breton Island, and Sable Island until they came to the mouth of the Mississippi Delta. They entered the Mississippi cleanly, and their first stop was a port town called Jump, Louisiana.

They took their time and made the Delta in eight hours. Moses was not in any hurry and told Captain Blowers so. It wasn't until they left New Orleans that he'd want the captain to show some speed.

It was about twenty-five miles from the Delta to Jump, and they did that in a leisurely couple of hours, even though Moses knew they could have done it much faster.

In Jump, Moses found the extra leadsman he was looking for. Clint, Laura, and Cinda did not even get off the boat, and they were under way again in the morning.

Moses was impressed with Blowers because he had made his way from the mouth of the Delta to Jump in the dark with no trouble. It was starting to look like the man knew his job, but there was still plenty of Mississippi to test him with.

And he would be tested.

• • •

From Jump to New Orleans was a six-hour trip, and by the time they arrived Laura and Cinda were itching to disembark and do some shopping.

"Don't be gone long, Laura," Moses warned her as the two women prepared to leave. "Your girls will be arriving soon."

"I'll be here to look over my girls, Mr. Moses," Laura said. "Don't you worry."

As they left, Clint asked, "How many girls are we talking about?"

"I don't know," Moses said. "I've got to go and find some. Want to help?"

"What? I thought you'd hired them already and they'd be waiting."

"Didn't have time," Moses said, "and I didn't want to trust it to anyone else. Are you game to look them over with me?"

"As long as we're only looking them over," Clint said, "and not trying them out."

"Well," Moses said, "we may have to try one or two, just to be on the safe side."

"Well," Clint replied, in kind, "better to be safe than sorry, I guess."

"That's my man!"

They went to three whorehouses in New Orleans, and Clint was not surprised to find that J. P. Moses was known—and most welcome—in all of them.

"You come to take one of my girls wit' you on your boat, *cher*?" Mama Tousseau asked, bumping him with her mammoth breasts. The woman was huge, but Clint noticed that she had flawless skin. In her younger days she might have been a real beauty.

"One girl, Mama, that's all," Moses said.

"Come you pick, den," she said, waving him into the parlor, where her girls were sitting, some alone, some with potential customers.

"Girls," Mama Tousseau called out, clapping her hands, "dis is de famous J. P. Moses, here. He come to take one of you away to work on his boat."

"In a boat?" one girl asked.

"A floating whorehouse?" another chimed in.

"There will be gambling, food, music, everything a man—or woman—could want on the *Biloxi Queen*," Moses announced. "Who wants to come?"

Three or four anxious girls raised their hands, but Clint knew that Moses had noticed the same woman he had. She was black, her skin fairly gleaming, tall and graceful with high, proud breasts and full luscious lips.

"What about you?" Moses asked the black woman.

Clint noticed her because she was somewhat older than the others, possibly the only woman—other than Mama Tousseau—who was over thirty.

"Why would I want to come on your boat?" the woman asked. Her voice was husky, the kind of voice that played a man's spine as if it was a musical instrument.

"Why not?" Moses asked.

"I need a better reason than that."

"Hey," another girl called out, "some of us want that job."

Moses turned to Clint.

"Why don't you stay here and talk to these women and I'll go on to the next place."

"Next place?" Mama asked. "What other place is there but Mama's?"

Moses stroked her cheek and said, "I have to be fair,

Mama. I have a lot of friends in New Orleans.''

"Sure you do," Mama said, laughing. "You come back here later, *cher*, I show you how friendly Mama can be." She shook her immense bosom at him and laughed.

Moses kissed Mama soundly, then waved at Clint and said, "See you at Lucky Lou's."

"I'll find it," Clint said.

"Mama can tell you how to get there."

As Moses left, Mama said to Clint, "Lucky Lou, she have cows compared to Mama's girls."

"Where can I talk to the girls, Mama?" he asked.

"What your name, *cher*?"

"Clint Adams."

"Adams?" Mama said, her eyes wide. "You as famous off the Mississippi as Mr. Moses is on, *non*?"

"I guess . . .''

"I take you to my room, you talk to the girls there. Which ones you wan' talk to?"

Clint pointed to three, and then the black woman as the fourth.

"You go up, first door on de left, and I send dem, no?"

"All right."

Clint went up the stairs, wondering what he'd gotten himself into. He hoped he wasn't expected to sample four whores in one afternoon—or one hour!

SEVENTEEN

The first three girls were pretty, and young, and all offered to let him "sample" their wares. In the end he let
them strip, two showing him their breasts and one taking
her clothes off completely and making it very hard for him
to resist.

And then the black woman entered.

"I got to sleep with you for this job?" she asked, tilting
her chin up and giving him a haughty look.

"No."

"Undress? Get naked for you to touch me? Look at
me?"

"No," he said, "I can see enough of you right now."

The gown she was wearing was cut low, showing off her
full breasts to their best advantage. She was tall, as tall as
Laura, but much slimmer. He wondered how she would get
along with Laura.

"And who would I work for?" she asked.

"Mr. Moses would pay you," he said, "but you would
be working for a woman named Laura Giles."

"Is she old, like Mama?"

"No," Clint said, "she's young, probably about your
age."

The woman smiled without showing any teeth.

"You think you can guess a black woman's age?"

"Why not?"

"Most white men can't."

"Well," Clint said, "I may be wrong, but you'll never see twenty-nine again."

"And?"

"And thirty-five is still a few years away."

"Hmph," she said. "Not bad."

"What's your name?"

"Ebony."

"Your real name."

She hesitated, then said, "Darla."

"I like that better."

"Me, too," Darla said. "Mama makes me use Ebony."

"You come with us, you can use your real name, or whatever name you want."

"How much is the pay?"

"I don't know," he said honestly, "but better than this, I'll bet."

"Are you a betting man?"

"I am."

"You famous or somethin'?" she asked.

"Why?"

"Mama said you were famous."

"You know Mr. Moses's name?"

"Sure, I know it," she said. "I been in New Orleans four months, I heard his name plenty."

"That's all you need to know."

"Why do you want me for your boat?"

"His boat," Clint said, "and I expect he wants you because you are unusually beautiful."

"Because I'm black?"

"I don't know," Clint said. "Is that why you're beautiful?"

"I don't look like any of the girls downstairs."

"What's it going to be, Darla?" Clint asked, finally pushing her. "Yes or no?"

"How long I got to decide?"

"As long as it takes me to walk downstairs and out the door."

"Okay, then," she said. "I'll come and work on your boat."

"Pack," he said, "and be down at the dock in two hours. Either I or Mr. Moses or Laura will be there to welcome you."

"That's it?" she asked.

"That's it."

"I don't have to have sex with you?"

"No."

"Or Mr. Moses?"

"That's between you and him," Clint said, "but the job doesn't rely on it."

"Two hours?"

"Two hours."

She hesitated a moment, then said, "I'll be there."

"Fine," he said. "You want to tell Mama, or shall I?"

"You tell her," Darla said. "I'm going right to my room to pack."

"Then I'll see you later."

"Hey?" she called as he headed for the door.

"Yes?"

"What do I call you?"

"You call me Clint."

"And what do I call Moses?"

"Oh," Clint said, "him you call Mr. Moses, unless he tells you otherwise."

"It's his boat, huh?"

Clint nodded, said, "It's his boat," and left the room to talk to Mama Tousseau.

The next stop for J. P. Moses was a huge establishment run by a woman named Angelique. She was easily in her eighties, thin as a rail, and only too happy to have one of her girls work on his boat.

"You give her back when you are done with her, no?"

"Yes," Moses said, "or when she's done with me."

"Fair," Angelique said. "I pick, yes?"

"Pick me a good one, Angelique."

The woman left and came back with a full-bosomed blonde in her mid-twenties, maybe five five, with blue-green eyes the color of the Atlantic Ocean. Moses knew because he'd seen it once.

"This is April."

"April, I'm J. P. Moses."

"I know who you are, sir."

"You don't have to call me sir."

April looked at Angelique and then at Moses.

"We call all our gentlemen sir . . . sir."

"Do you want to work for me?"

"Yes, sir."

"Then you'll call me Mr. Moses."

"Yes, Mr. Moses."

"Pack and be on the *Biloxi Queen* in two hours." He told her the same thing Clint had told Darla, that he, Clint, or Laura would be there to welcome her.

"Thank you, si—Mr. Moses."

"That's quite all right, April," Moses said. "You're very beautiful."

"Thank you."

Moses kissed Angelique's withered, powdered cheek and said, "You're an angel."

"I know," she said, as he went out the door. The last thing he heard her say to April was "Scoot! Pack!"

EIGHTEEN

Clint arrived at Lucky Lou's before Moses and decided to wait on the porch for him. Mama had given him directions, and a warning.

"Lucky Lou's on Bourbon Street," she said. "You watch yourself there, yes?"

"I'll be careful," he promised.

Clint had been to Bourbon Street before, but never to Lucky Lou's. It was a huge house with a courtyard behind a wrought iron gate, and it took up half the block.

"Can't get in?" Moses asked, joining him by the gate.

"Haven't tried yet," Clint said. "I was waiting for you."

"Which girl did you get?"

"The black one."

"Try her out?"

"No."

"How'd she look naked?"

"I don't know."

"You hired her without trying her or getting a look at her?"

"You would have, too."

Moses stared at him a moment and then smiled and said, "You're right. Come on, let's go inside."

There was a bellpull on the right side of the gate, and Moses gave it a yank. They couldn't hear anything, but someone did, because a black butler appeared and unlocked the door.

"Good to see you again, Mr. Moses."

"Thank you, Gunner. This is my friend, Clint Adams."

"Pleased to meet you, suh."

Gunner had a pronounced Southern accent and was no doubt an ex-slave. He still shuffled when he walked, as if he still wore chains, even almost twenty years after being freed.

"Come this way, suhs."

Moses leaned over and said into Clint's ear, "He never calls *anyone* 'gentlemen.' "

"Probably comes from having been owned by a few men who called themselves that."

Clint thought he'd been speaking low enough to go unheard, but Gunner dispelled that when he turned and said to him, "You is right about that, suh."

Clint remained silent the rest of the way, until they were in the house.

"If you will wait here . . ." Gunner said.

"Sure, Gunner."

As the black man left, Clint said, "So who is Lucky Lou?"

"Ever heard of Lou Diamond Racine?"

"Racine?" Clint said, looking surprised. "Lou Racine was one of the top gamblers in the country, until he disappeared ten years ago."

"Didn't disappear," Moses said. "He bought this place, and he stays holed up inside."

"Why?"

"Because he was so good at what he did that he never lost," Moses said. "Never. I'm good, but I lose once in a while, Clint. What about Bat Masterson? Luke Short?"

"They've been known to lose a time or two, probably to each other."

"I know," Moses said, "I've beaten them and lost to each of them myself. But Racine? He never lost."

"How can that be?"

"That's what people started asking," Moses said, "and some of them wanted to ask with guns. In the end he was a marked man, so he came here and . . . well, let's say he retired."

"To run a whorehouse?"

"A whorehouse, and gambling parlor."

"Does he play himself?"

"Never."

"That's a shame."

"Not really," Moses said, "because in owning this place, he still never loses."

Gunner returned and said, "Mr. Racine will see you now, suhs."

They followed him.

NINETEEN

"Mr. Moses," Racine said, extending his hand. "What a surprise."

Racine was tall and slender, probably in his late forties. His dark hair was slick and shiny, and came to a sharp widow's peak. He was impeccably dressed. His face was odd, broad at the forehead and then narrowing down to a pointy chin. His eyebrows were full and arched, forming a *V* over his eyes.

Gunner had led them down a hall, away from the action. The only hints of what was going on in other rooms were the sound of chips hitting each other, the smell of cigarette and cigar smoke, the sound of voices, and the smell of many different varieties of perfume.

"And who is this gentleman?" Racine asked.

"Lou, this is Clint Adams, a good friend of mine."

"Ah," Racine said, raising one eyebrow, "I know Mr. Adams by reputation only. It's my pleasure to meet you, sir."

Clint shook hands and said, "Mine, too."

"Have you gentlemen come to play?"

"I'm afraid not, Lou," Moses said. "I've got a new boat docked here, and I need a girl."

"One girl?"

"Just one."

"And do I know what you need her for?"

"You can figure it out."

"And you want me to give you one, for free?"

"Not for free," Moses said. "I want to give one of them an opportunity. She'll make a good wage."

"Ah," Racine said, "but what will I get?"

"The satisfaction of knowing that one of your girls has gone on to another adventure."

They were in Racine's office and he walked around behind his desk and sat down. Two walls, to their right and left, were covered with books. The wall behind his desk had one window. There were no paintings anywhere, or any other decorations.

Clint noticed that on the desktop, to Racine's right, was a deck of cards. It was obviously well used.

"What do you want in return, Lou?"

"Have you gone to the other places in the city?"

"Two of them."

"Angelique?"

Moses nodded.

"Don't tell me," Racine said, raising a hand. "Mama's."

"Right again."

"Only the best for Mr. Moses."

"That's my reputation."

Racine sat back, steepled his fingers in front of his face, and regarded Clint and Moses over them.

"I do have a girl who might suit you."

"Good."

"Are you a partner, Mr. Adams?"

"No," Clint said. "I'm just along for the ride."

"What do you think I should get in return?"

"I don't know," Clint said. "The others didn't ask for anything."

"Ah, but they were women."

"What's your point?"

"They were charmed by your friend, Mr. Moses."

"I see. You're not charmed?"

"Not enough to give up something for nothing."

"I see," Clint said again. He looked at the deck of cards pointedly. "May I?"

"Of course."

"Are you still a gambling man, Mr. Racine?"

"Occasionally," Racine said, "and behind these walls only."

"Well, then, why don't you and Mr. Moses cut for it?"

"Cut for what?"

"The girl you mentioned."

"Ah," Racine said, "but what do I get if I win?"

"Me."

"I beg your pardon?"

"You get me," Clint said, "as a bodyguard, for a week when we come back downriver."

"Why would I need you as a bodyguard?"

"I understand you stay behind these walls for your safety."

"That's true."

"When's the last time you went out, saw the city?"

"I really can't remember."

"Well, if you win I'll take you out into the city and guarantee your safety. You'll get to go outside these walls for a change."

Racine seemed to be considering the proposal.

"Do you approve of this, Mr. Moses?"

"Sure, Lou," Moses said. "It's Clint's time."

Racine regarded his steepled fingers for a few moments.

"Do you want to see the girl?"

"I trust your judgment, Lou," Moses said.

"All right, then," Racine said. "We'll cut."

Clint put the cards on the desk.

"Who goes first?" Moses asked.

"First," Racine said, "we'll need someone to cut them."

"Why?" Moses asked.

"I believe you are as capable as I am, Mr. Moses, of pulling an ace out of that deck."

"Are you saying I'd cheat?"

"I'm saying why risk it?"

"If you both pull aces," Clint said, "nobody wins."

"And nobody loses," Racine said.

"So I'll cut."

"I believe you know your way around a deck of cards, Mr. Adams," Racine said. "At least, that's what I've heard."

"Who, then?" Clint asked.

"Gunner?"

"He's your man," Moses said.

"Are you saying my man would cheat?"

Moses smiled.

"I'm saying why take the risk?"

"All right," Clint said, "who, then?"

Racine thought a moment.

"The girl?"

"Your girl," Moses pointed out.

"She won't know why she's cutting," Racine said, "and she won't know who she is cutting for. The first cut will be for you, and the second for me."

"How about the other way around?" Clint asked.

"Fine," Racine said. "I'll have Gunner bring her in."

As if on cue Gunner appeared at the door, opening it, closing it behind him, and then approaching the desk.

"Suh?"

"Bring in Marianne, Gunner."

"Yes, suh."

After Gunner had left the room, Racine looked at them and asked, "Port?"

TWENTY

The three men had some very good port while they waited for Gunner to return with the girl.

"Tell me about the girl," Moses said at one point.

"You'll see when she gets here," Racine said. "I don't think you'll be disappointed. Why don't you tell me about this new boat. Have you given up the *Dead Man's Chance*?"

Moses explained that the *Biloxi Queen* was a second boat and would not replace the first, the *Dead Man's Chance*. He was finishing up his explanation when there was a gentle knock at the door.

"Come in," Racine called out.

The door opened and a girl entered. She was small, perhaps an inch or two taller than Cinda Wolfe, and she appeared to be about twenty, if that. Her gown did not reveal much in the way of cleavage, but it didn't have to. All three men watched her as she walked across the room, and the closer she got the more beautiful she became. She had dark lustrous hair and pale luminous skin. Her eyes were huge and dark.

"Didn't I tell you?" Racine said to Moses. "Gentlemen, this is Marianne."

"A pleasure," she said to both men. "Mr. Racine? Gunner said you wanted to see me?" Her voice had a breathless quality that would have men leaning in to hear her.

"Yes, Marianne," Racine said. "I need your help."

"Of course. W-what is it you would like me to do?"

"I need you to cut two cards from this deck, Marianne."

"Cut?" She didn't understand the word.

"Take two cards out of the deck and place them face-down on the desk."

"Take them from the top?"

"Discard the top card, then take the others from any-where in the deck except the bottom," Moses instructed her.

She looked at Racine.

"Do it."

"All right."

The deck had already been shuffled by all three men. She took the first card from the top and set it aside, then took two more cards from different parts of the deck and set them down on the desk. All three men knew clearly which card was Moses's and which was Racine's.

"Is that all, Mr. Racine?"

"For now," Racine said, "but I might need you again in a little while, so don't disappear, all right?"

"Yes, sir." She turned to Clint and Moses and said, "Gentlemen."

"Thank you for your help, Marianne," Moses said.

"It was my pleasure."

They watched her until she disappeared through the door.

"Exquisite, isn't she?" Racine asked.

"Very," Moses said.

"Let's do it," Clint said, looking at the cards on the desk.

"Pick up your card, Mr. Moses," Racine said.

Moses picked up his and Racine did the same.

"Let's put them down together," Racine said, "now."

They set the cards down on the desk. Racine had the king of hearts. Moses had the ace of spades.

"Amazing," Racine said.

Clint thought so, too.

"She's yours."

"If she wants to be," Moses said. "If she refuses . . ."

"You can pick any girl you want and offer them the job," Racine said. "I wouldn't want to cut you for each girl, I might lose my whole stable."

"Thanks, Lou."

Racine waved a hand and then looked at Clint.

"Mr. Adams, I'd like to hire you to do what you said you'd do if Mr. Moses lost."

"I'm sorry," Clint said, "but I don't hire out."

"But—"

"I was just trying to help Mr. Moses," Clint said. "If he'd lost I would have abided by the bet, but I don't hire my gun out."

"I see," Racine said. "You did what you did out of friendship."

"Yes."

"Well," Racine said, "perhaps one day we'll be friends."

"When we are," Clint said, "ask me again."

"Very well. Mr. Moses, always a pleasure."

The two men shook hands.

"Gunner will take you to a room where you can talk to Marianne and make your offer."

Moses said thanks again and he and Clint left the office.

Marianne jumped at the opportunity. It seemed she didn't really like working at Lucky Lou's. They instructed her to be at the boat in two hours' time, but she asked if she could leave with them.

"Don't you have to pack?" Moses asked.

"I don't have much," she said. "One suitcase, and I always keep it half packed."

Obviously, she'd been looking for a chance to leave Lucky Lou's. Did Racine know this? Was that why he chose her?

"All right, Marianne," Moses said, "we'll wait for you in the front hall."

"Thank you."

"What do you suppose that's about?" Moses asked as the girl went to pack.

"Who knows?" Clint asked. "And what's the difference? You've got yourself three girls. Is that going to be enough?"

"We can pick some more up along the way," Moses said. "That's enough from New Orleans."

Marianne returned fifteen minutes later, and she had not only packed, but she had changed her clothes. She was wearing a purple shirt, black pants, and boots.

"I'm ready."

"Don't you want to say good-bye to anyone?" Moses asked.

"No. I'm ready."

"All right, then," Moses said. "Let's go."

Gunner showed the three of them out.

"It was nice seeing you again, Gunner," Moses said.

"You, too, Mr. Moses, Mr. Adams."

"Bye, Gunner," Marianne said.

"Good-bye, miss."

As Gunner went back inside, Marianne said, "You

know, he's the only person in that house I could trust.''

''Why's that?'' Moses asked.

''He's the only one who didn't want something from me.''

Clint wondered if she would find someone on the *Biloxi Queen* she would feel the same way about.

TWENTY-ONE

Darla and April arrived about an hour after Clint and Moses returned with Marianne. Moses waited until then to introduce the three girls to Laura.

"Laura will be in charge of you," he explained.

"She's the madam?" Darla asked.

"I guess you could call me that," Laura said.

"How old are you?" Darla asked.

Laura smiled at the three girls and said, "We can discuss things like that while I show you to your cabins."

"We'll be getting under way in about an hour," Moses told them. "Don't leave the boat."

"They won't," Laura said. "Follow me, ladies."

All four women left the dining room, and Moses looked at Clint.

"You want to eat something?"

"Sure, why not?"

They had something that was a cross between lunch and dinner. One of the waiters brought it out from the kitchen for them. It consisted of bread and cold chicken.

"When will the gambling start?" Clint asked.

"I left instructions with Mr. Bixby to start booking passengers," Moses said. "In fact, I'd better check to see how many we got. As soon as we leave the dock, I'll open the tables."

"Where's the *Dead Man's Chance* about now?"

"That's the best part," Moses said. "It'll be leaving St. Paul just about now. We should pass each other at the half-way point."

"When do the girls start working?"

"Laura should have them ready by tonight."

"Think she'll have any trouble handling them?" Clint asked.

"If she can handle what's her name, Ebony?"

"Darla," Clint said. "Mama insisted she use the name Ebony. She hates it."

"Well, if she can handle Darla, she'll be able to handle anyone."

They finished up their meal and prepared to leave the dining room.

"The three of them are beautiful, aren't they?" Moses asked.

"Yes, they are."

"And in very different ways," Moses said. "I think we did a good job together, Clint. What Lou asked about you being a partner? Maybe we should consider that."

"Maybe we shouldn't," Clint said. "I'm just along for the ride, remember? I'm going to be too busy gambling to handle a floating whorehouse."

"It's not a floating whorehouse," Moses protested.

"I know."

They walked out on deck together.

"I think you're going to be busy with Cinda," Moses said.

"Maybe."

"You're not going to want to try these girls out?" Moses asked.

"I don't know."

"Take my advice. Don't stick to one woman, Clint," Moses said. "You'll give her ideas."

"What about Laura?"

"Laura works for me. She knows that. There won't be any problems there."

"For your sake," Clint said, "I hope so."

TWENTY-TWO

Clint went with Moses to check with Mr. Bixby on how many passengers they had. They had filled half the boat, and they still had plenty of stops to make.

"By the time we get to St. Paul," Moses said, "we should have a full house."

"Looks like more passengers, Mr. Moses," Mr. Bixby said.

Clint and Moses both looked down at the dock and saw half a dozen men approaching.

"The law," Moses said.

"How do you know?"

"The fella in the lead is Lieutenant Pat Cummings."

"You know him," Clint said, then asked, "does he know you?"

"He thinks he does."

"What's that mean?"

Moses looked at Clint.

"Come with me and listen while I talk to him and you'll see."

"Lead the way."

Clint and Moses reached the gangplank at the same time Lieutenant. Cummings was boarding. His five men were waiting on the dock for him.

"Pat," Moses said, "nice to see you."

"Mr. Moses."

The two men did not shake hands. Clint was constantly surprised by how many people—Lou Racine, even this policeman—referred to Moses as "Mr." as if that was his first name.

"Gonna join us going upriver, Pat?" Moses asked.

"Don't think I can get the time off," Cummings said. He was well-dressed, clean-shaven, his hair freshly shorn. He looked to be in his thirties.

"What can I do for you, then?"

"I want to search your boat, Mr. Moses."

Moses frowned.

"What for?"

"I'll tell you that after I search," Cummings said. "Have you got something to hide?"

"No, no," Moses said, "nothing. Search away, but be quick about it, will you, Pat? I want to get under way."

"We'll be as quick as we can be," Cummings said.

"Take it easy on the passengers, will you? I don't want them chased off before we even get going."

Cummings smiled, but Clint noticed that it didn't reach his eyes.

"Don't worry, I won't scare them away before you can take some of their money."

"Appreciate it, Pat."

The policeman turned and waved to his men, and they swarmed onboard and began to search.

"Who is this gentleman?" Cummings asked.

"Lieutenant Pat Cummings," Moses said, making the introductions, "meet Clint Adams."

"*The* Clint Adams?" The lieutenant caught himself but not before it was evident that he was impressed.

"The only one I know of," Clint said. "A pleasure, Lieutenant." He followed Moses's example and did not offer to shake hands.

"I take it you're not just another passenger, Mr. Adams?"

"Actually, I am," Clint said, "but if you mean to ask if Mr. Moses and I are friends, the answer is yes."

"I see."

"Care to tell me what you're looking for, Pat?" Moses asked. "Or are you just trying to catch me with something?"

"When I do catch you it will be with something, don't you worry."

"I'll worry when you stop trying to catch me with something, Pat."

The lieutenant's men searched for an hour. During that time Clint, Moses, and Cummings remained on deck. The lieutenant turned down coffee, beer, and cognac.

In turn each of his men returned and shook their heads, then walked down the gangplank. After the fifth man had departed, Cummings turned to Moses.

"We had a tip we'd find some dead men onboard, Mr. Moses," Cummings said.

"And did you?"

"You know we didn't. It looks like somebody's trying to cause you some trouble, my friend. I'd be careful if I were you."

"I'm always careful, Pat."

Cummings paused before leaving.

"I'm glad this tip didn't pay off. When I catch you I want it to be because I got the goods on you myself, not because I got a tip and somebody framed you."

"I'd expect nothing less from you, Pat."

Cummings looked at Clint, said, "Good day," nodded to Moses, and followed his men.

"And what was that about?" Clint asked.

"Masters," Moses said. "He must have tipped the police about the men he sent onboard in Biloxi. I don't know why he'd think we'd keep their bodies onboard."

"I guess they haven't surfaced yet," Clint said, "but I meant the song and dance you just did with your friend there."

"Pat's not my friend. He's not a bad guy, though. If he wasn't so convinced that I was dirty I think we probably could be friends."

"Why is he so convinced?"

"I've never been able to find that out," Moses said. "He's been after me for a couple of years now, and damned if I know why."

"You don't seem to mind."

Moses looked at him.

"Why should I mind? He's doing his job. Besides, he's not going to catch me doing anything I'm not supposed to be doing, is he?"

"I hope not."

Moses slapped Clint on the back and said, "We're gonna get under way. You better go inside and pick out a game."

Clint watched Moses walk away and then turned to watch Lieutenant Cummings and his men leave the dock area. He searched the dock with his eyes, wondering if whoever had tipped them off was there somewhere, watching. Had Captain Masters sent a message by telegraph? Or had he come to New Orleans himself to cause trouble for Moses? He certainly could have beaten them there by land route.

Clint remained where he was until two men hauled in the gangplank and the boat started to move. He noticed that one of the men was the fellow who had swabbed the blood off the deck in Biloxi. Had the lawmen questioned anyone? he wondered. Or had they simply searched? And was this going to happen at every port they stopped in?

That remained to be seen.

TWENTY-THREE

Clint did not pick out a game right away. He preferred to watch J. P. Moses's operation in action. He walked around, watching the people gamble. It looked to him as if Moses had staffed his boat with experienced dealers and croupiers. All of the tables were running smoothly. He stopped to put some chips on numbers at two of the roulette wheels, lost, and moved on.

At one point he stopped to watch Cinda Wolfe deal blackjack. She was smooth and expert. She saw him watching and graced him with a single smile, then ignored him, paying attention to her work.

"She's very good, isn't she?"

He turned and saw Laura standing next to him, looking lovely and sophisticated in a gown that showed much of her cleavage, but not as much as you'd see on a saloon girl.

"You look beautiful."

"Thank you, sir."

"And yes, she is very good. How are your girls doing?"

"Oh, they'll be up a little later to circulate," she assured him.

"How are you getting along with them?"

"Oh, I'm doing well with two out of three, but the third will come along."

"Darla?"

Laura hesitated, then smiled and nodded.

"She has a little bit of an attitude."

"I noticed."

"You recruited her?"

"Yes."

"A good choice," Laura said. "I think of the three she'll do the most business."

"Even though she's black?"

"That won't matter on the Mississippi," Laura said. "Here a woman is a woman, and she is all woman. She's stunning."

"Well . . . thanks for approving."

"Moses picked April, didn't he?"

"Yes, he did."

"I thought so. And Marianne?"

"We went to Lou Racine and he chose her."

Laura looked surprised. She had obviously heard of Racine.

"Three women picked by three different men," she said. "I approve of the way you and he handled this."

"Is three enough?" Clint asked.

"Not if the boat fills up," Laura said. "I understand that our Mr. Moses will continue to recruit along the way. I hope he also continues to allow you to help. You have good taste."

"Thanks."

She started away, then turned back.

"By the way," she said, "my ladies have a very high opinion of you."

"Is that a fact?"

"I'd appreciate it if you didn't . . . play with them during working hours."

Clint grinned.

"I see you're going to be a harsh task . . . mistress?"

"That's what I'm getting paid for," she said, and glided away. Clint was impressed with the way she moved for a large woman.

He left Cinda to her work and continued to roam the boat. Moses had left two tables free for private poker games, games that would not have a house dealer. Both of those tables were empty at the moment. There were five house game tables, and three of those were in use. Clint stood at a distance that was too far for him to see players' cards, but not too far for him to watch the dealers. From what he could see, they were all dealing fairly.

"What do you think?" Moses asked, coming up behind him.

"Very nice operation, Jack."

"Catch anybody bottom dealing?"

"Nope."

"Good. I hate having to fire people first time out."

"Everything is on the up-and-up, isn't it, Jack?" Clint asked.

"What a question," Moses said. "Of course it is. The house has enough of an advantage without cheating, don't you think?"

"Yes, I do," Clint said, "but I've met a lot of casino owners who don't agree. I'm glad that you do."

"Have you played yet?"

"A couple of numbers on the roulette wheel," Clint said. "I'm in no hurry."

"I saw you talking to Laura."

"She's having some trouble with Darla."

"Maybe I should talk to her."

"If you want my advice," Clint said, "I'd say no. You hired Laura to handle the girls, let her handle them."

"I'll take that advice," Moses said, "and raise you a drink."

"I accept."

They walked over to the bar, and the bartender gave them each a beer.

"You've got him trained already," Clint said.

"Eric, meet Clint."

The bartender, a handsome young man in his late twenties or early thirties, reached across the bar to shake Clint's hand.

"A pleasure. Is beer your drink?"

"When I'm not gambling, yeah."

"Well, I've got my instructions from the boss, here."

"And what are they?"

"You drink on the house."

Clint grinned.

"He's just trying to keep me too drunk to gamble and win."

"I don't have to keep you drunk to beat you."

"Don't listen to him," Clint said to Eric. "The man's having delusions."

"Are you saying I can't beat you?" Moses asked.

"At what?"

"You pick the game."

"You're a businessman, Jack," Clint said. "You can't be participating in private games."

"Sure I can," Moses said. "I've even got a private room for it."

"Well," Clint said, "find four other players who can stay with you and me and we'll play."

"Well, forget it, then," Moses said.

"Hey, boss," Eric said, "you gonna let him get away with that?"

"Eric," Moses said, "there aren't four other players on this boat who could sit at the same table with Clint and me."

"Maybe we'll pick somebody else up along the way," Clint said.

"I hope so," Eric said. "I'd like to see that."

"You," Moses said, pointing at Eric, "get paid to stay behind the bar."

Moses finished up his beer and said to Clint, "I've got to circulate. Seriously, Clint, if you see something you don't like, let me know."

"I will, don't worry."

"Something you don't like?" Eric asked. "Like what?"

"Cheating."

"Whoa," the bartender said. "What happens if he catches somebody cheating?"

"That depends."

"On what?"

"On whether it's a patron," Clint said, "or an employee."

TWENTY-FOUR

Clint remained at the bar for a while, getting to know Eric. As it turned out, the man had been tending bar for a few years but had never worked on a boat.

"Mr. Moses came into a saloon I was working in in Baton Rouge and hired me on the spot."

"I guess he liked what he saw," Clint said. "By the way, you do pour a mean beer."

"Another?"

"Nope," Clint said, putting the empty mug down, "I think I'll circulate, too."

"You never answered my question."

"Which question was that?"

"What happens if Mr. Moses catches somebody cheating?"

"If it's a patron, they get blackballed and put off at the next port."

"And if it's an employee?"

Clint smiled.

"They get put off, immediately."

"You mean—"

"I mean," Clint said, "they better know how to swim."

He walked away from the bar, leaving Eric with his mouth hanging open.

• • •

The man watched J. P. Moses and Clint Adams at the bar as they shared a beer, and then Moses walked away. From his vantage point he could still watch the two men, even though they had separated.

He knew Moses's reputation on the river, and understood that he was a dangerous man in many ways—both on a gaming table and off.

It was Clint Adams, however, who the man felt was the more lethal of the two. It had been said that Moses had chucked more than one man off of his boats, leaving them to brave the Mississippi—in which case he might or might not have actually killed them.

With Clint Adams, however, there was no doubt that he had killed many men. Since the man himself had killed, he knew instinctively that Clint Adams was the danger to him, but that didn't mean he wouldn't be wary of Mr. Moses.

When he'd been hired, it had only been to deal with Moses, so before the man took any action—now that he knew Clint Adams was involved—he was going to have to arrange for more money. That meant getting off the boat at the next port that had a telegraph office and making arrangements for an increase in pay.

"Sir?"

He became aware that the pretty red-haired dealer was talking to him.

"Hmm? I'm sorry."

"Do you want a card?"

"Oh," the man said, looking down at his hand, "hit me, please."

TWENTY-FIVE

When Cinda took a break, Clint sat down at a table with her and had a drink.

"How's it going?" he asked.

"Very well," she said, "but you'd think people would concentrate when they have their money on the table."

"Oh? Somebody losing carelessly?"

"Lots of people lose," Cinda said. "In fact, most of them lose, but usually it's because they're bad players."

"Uh-huh," he said, figuring she'd get to the point sooner or later.

"There's this man who's not a bad player, but his concentration keeps wandering. He took a hit on an eighteen just a minute ago because he wasn't paying attention to his cards."

"Whoa," Clint said, "that's a sure way to lose your money."

"Well, usually," she said sheepishly.

"Usually?"

"He drew a three for twenty-one and beat my twenty."

"Ah, I see," Clint said. "We've got some hurt pride here."

She grinned sheepishly.

"Maybe that's it. How are you doing?"

"I'm doing good."

"Have you gambled yet?"

"No."

"Why not?"

"The time has to be just right."

"Come over to my table."

"Why?"

"I want to see how good you are."

"If anybody knows how good I am," Clint said, "it's you."

She slapped his wrist and said, "You know what I mean."

"Blackjack's not my game," he said. "I prefer poker."

"But you know how to play blackjack, don't you?"

"Of course."

"Then come and play at my table."

"Why? So you can take my money?"

"Maybe."

"Hey," Clint said, leaning forward, "you could deal me winning hands and we could split the money."

She gave him a look of mock horror.

"Do you know what you're suggesting?" she asked. "I could get fired."

"So what? We'd have enough money so you wouldn't have to work."

"And we'd stay together?" she asked. "With all that money?"

"Sure."

"And have children?"

"Sure."

"And raise them together?"

"Sure."

"You're full of—"

"Sure."

She smiled and pushed her chair back.

"I have to get back to work," she said. "Come on over when you get a chance."

"Sure."

She laughed and walked away. Clint remained where he was, finishing his drink.

"Looking for company, mister?"

He looked up and saw the black woman, Darla, standing there.

"Aren't you supposed to work the paying customers?" he asked.

She looked stunning. She was wearing a dress that left her shoulders bare and revealed plenty of chocolaty cleavage.

"I just thought I'd practice on you."

"Are the other girls around, also?"

"Yes," she said. "We're all working."

"How do you like it so far?"

"I'm curious."

"About what?"

"About what men want more," she said, "gambling or sex."

"Well," he said, "if anyone was ever in a position to satisfy their curiosity it's you."

"Want to help me?" she asked. "Which do you prefer?"

"Looking at you right now," he said, "I think the answer would be obvious."

"Darla," Laura Giles said, coming up next to the dark woman, "the paying customers are waiting."

Darla gave Laura a long, slow look and asked innocently, "Isn't he a paying customer?"

"No," Laura said, "he's a friend of the owner."

"Really?" Darla looked at Clint. "How dare you impersonate a paying customer. Shame on you.''

She gave him a smile and walked away.

"Did you ask her over?"

"Actually, no," Clint said. "She came over on her own.
I think she was just making conversation. How are you two
getting along?"

"It's coming along," Laura said, "slowly. Mind if I
sit?"

"Are you allowed?" Clint asked. "What about the paying customers?"

"My girls take care of them," Laura said, sitting opposite him. "I take care of the friends of the owner."

"And the owner?"

She smiled and said, "Him, too."

At that point they both looked across the room and saw
Moses talking to April, who gave all the appearances of a
girl who was working a paying customer.

"But maybe not for long," Laura added.

"He's only talking to her, Laura."

Laura took her eyes off of Moses and April and looked
at Clint.

"It's all right," she said. "I knew it wouldn't last. He's
under no obligation, anyway. If he comes to my room tonight, fine, if not . . . that's fine, too. Excuse me, I have to
get to work."

"Laura—" he started as she stood up.

"It's all right, Clint," she said, "really. I know J. P.
Moses is not a one-woman man."

"Well—"

"I just hope Cinda knows the same thing about you."

"Hey—"

"It's okay," she said, cutting him off again. "Most men
are that way. It's okay, really."

"Laura, just let me—"

"I have to go to work," she said, and walked away.

Clint wasn't at all sure he liked being lumped in with "most" men, but she was right about one thing. Moses was under no obligation to keep coming to her room every night. If she knew that, why was she so upset?

TWENTY-SIX

Later in the evening Clint found himself at the bar again with J. P. Moses. Since he and Laura saw Moses talking to April he had also seen the man talking to Marianne, and to Darla. In all instances their demeanor had been flirtatious—but then hadn't he and Darla been flirting, as well?

"Find a game yet?" Moses asked as Clint approached the bar. The bartender, Eric, immediately put down a beer for Clint.

"Thanks, Eric." He picked up the beer. "No game yet, Jack. I think I might have to wait until you have more customers."

"The roulette wheels are doing real well," Moses said happily.

"And the other tables?"

"I think faro may have seen its day," the gambler said, "but the blackjack tables are doing well, especially Cinda's."

"I thought it might," Clint said. "I noticed there hasn't been an empty seat there all night, except when she's taking a nap."

"I've noticed, too," Moses said. "She's going to be worth every penny I pay her."

"Maybe even worth a raise?"

"Well," Moses said, "let's not jump to conclusions."

•   •   •

Clint and Moses talked some more about the "operation," all the while unaware that they were being watched.

The man watching them was sitting at Cinda's table, once again making a mistake. He took a hit on nineteen and drew a three to bust—much to her relief. Still, she wondered what he was looking at when he wasn't looking at his cards. If he wanted to watch people, why didn't he just sit at a table and do that?

She took a second to try to follow his gaze. It seemed as if he was watching the bar. There were a few people standing there, ordering drinks or finishing drinks they had ordered. Among them were Clint Adams and J. P. Moses, not to mention the bartender, Eric, who was kind of cute.

"Mister?" she said to the man.

"Huh?"

"She wants you to bet," one of the other three players said, "and so do we, so we can get on with the game."

The man, who was sitting in the first chair, said, "Oh, sorry," and put up his bet.

The others bet and Cinda dealt. The man got an ace and then a king.

"Blackjack," Cinda said, shaking her head and paying the man off.

"What do you know about that?" the man asked, and collected his winnings.

"Yeah," she said, "what do you know?"

TWENTY-SEVEN

They stopped in Baton Rouge and Concordia before they reached Natchez. Moses told Clint that they'd be in Natchez for a full day.

"What for?"

"To pick up more talent."

"Women?"

Moses nodded, looking down at the dock as his men secured the *Biloxi Queen* in Natchez.

"More girls for Laura?"

Moses shook his head.

"We need girls to work the room, serve drinks, keep the patrons happy *without* sex. Laura and her girls will still take care of that."

"Why Natchez?"

"I've got a friend here who guaranteed me girls who would work hard."

"You have friends in every port up and down the Mississippi, Jack."

"That's true," Moses said, "but remember, I've got enemies, too."

"Do you want me to come along?"

"Why not?" Moses asked. "You did a great job in New Orleans, didn't you?"

"Considering the success the three girls have been, yes, I did."

"Meet me on the dock in an hour," Moses said. "I've got some other business to take care of. We're running low on some supplies."

They both left the bridge, Clint to go back to his cabin until he was to meet Moses. On the way there, though, he ran into Darla.

"Are you going ashore?" she asked.

"Yes, I am. You?"

She shook her head. She was wearing a man's shirt and a pair of jeans, and she looked just as stunning as she did when she was working. Her hair was down instead of up, and Clint found that he liked it better this way.

"I don't know anybody in Natchez. There's no reason for me to go ashore."

"What about shopping?"

"I got everything I need. The others are going, though."

"How are you getting along with Laura these days?"

Darla shrugged.

"She's all right. I've worked for worse people."

"And you get along with the other girls?"

"Sure," Darla said. "We're all out for the same thing."

"Which is what?"

"A living."

"Where are you off to?"

"Just thought I'd go on deck and look around," she said. "I'll see you later."

He nodded and waved, and she swept past him. He knew for a fact that while the other girls went ashore at each stop, she remained onboard. He also knew that while Moses had slept with April and Marianne already, he still had not slept with Darla, and he knew it was the black girl's choice.

"She's got that right," Moses even told him one night while they were drinking together, "but I'd sure like to give her a try. What about you?"

"Sure, I'd like to."

"Haven't yet?"

"No."

"And the others?"

"No."

"Still seeing Cinda?"

"Yes. What about you and Laura?"

"Laura's a little miffed with me, I think," Moses said, "but she'll get over it. We have a purely business relationship now."

"That's good," Clint said, although he wasn't sure how Laura felt about it. She didn't talk about Moses anymore, except as her boss.

Clint was happy seeing Cinda each evening. She was beautiful, intelligent, fun, and—above all—very understanding.

"You know," she told him one night while they were in bed, "you're free to do what you want."

"What's that mean?"

"You know," she said. "The other girls."

"What about them?"

"Come on," she said, "you must know they're interested in you."

"Are they?"

"Especially Darla."

"That's a surprise."

"Why?"

"She doesn't seem all that sociable."

"She keeps to herself," Cinda said. "I know she doesn't

shop with the other girls. To tell you the truth, I don't think she likes women much.''

''I got the impression she didn't like people much.''

''Maybe,'' Cinda said, ''but I know she's interested in you.''

''How can you tell?''

''I see the way she watches you.''

''Maybe it's your imagination.''

''I don't think so.''

''Well, I wouldn't worry about it.''

''I'm not worried,'' she said.

''And you wouldn't care if I slept with her?''

''No.''

''You're not the jealous type?''

''Oh, I am,'' she said. ''I mean, if you told me you were my man and I said I was your woman, then I'd be jealous.''

''But we haven't said that, have we?''

''No, we haven't.''

''So . . . you've seen someone else?''

She laughed.

''No, I haven't. I'm satisfied the way things are, for now.''

''Well, so am I.''

''Good.''

Alone in his cabin Clint thought about what Cinda had said. Darla did seem to make a habit of talking to him. He ran into her many times, both when she was working and when she wasn't. Was this by her design? Had he been too dense to notice it before now? If she was so standoffish to the others, why not to him? Was it a sexual thing? He didn't think so. If it was, she probably would have approached him by now. And if she did, could he resist? She was, after all, an amazing-looking woman—but for Clint, looks weren't everything. He liked Cinda because he could talk to her.

Then again, he could talk to Darla, too. In fact, all they'd *done* so far was talk.

Maybe Cinda was just seeing things.

He decided to go out on deck and wait for Moses, rather than sit in his cabin thinking about things that might not even be happening.

TWENTY-EIGHT

Moses took Clint to several restaurants in Natchez, but they didn't eat at any of them. Instead, Moses shopped for young waitresses that he could turn into saloon girls.

"Why not shop for them in saloons, then?" Clint asked as they walked from one restaurant to another. He was starting to wish that Moses had stopped to let them eat in one of the places.

"I don't want anyone who's already experienced," he explained to Clint. "I want some new blood."

"I would think you'd have less trouble with experienced girls, Jack."

"There won't be any trouble, Clint," Moses explained, "because I'll explain to these girls exactly what they have to do."

"Which is?"

"Serve drinks," Moses said, "flirt a little. Maybe get the customers worked up so that Laura and her girls can come in and make some money."

"And that's all?"

"That's all. They don't have to do any hard work. That will still be left to Laura and April and the others—plus they get to ride up and down the Mississippi on a riverboat owned by Mr. Moses. Who would turn me down?"

Who, indeed? As it turned out, the first half dozen girls

he faced all accepted the job. The owners they were working for at the time didn't like it, but there was no time for the girls to give them any kind of notice. They had to be on the *Biloxi Queen* by that night, or before morning when it departed.

All of the girls agreed.

"What do you think?" Moses asked Clint as they left the sixth and final restaurant. "They're all pretty, huh?"

"You have good taste in women, Jack, there's no denying that."

"And I don't think any of them are over twenty-five."

"I'd have to agree there, too."

"So, do you have a problem?"

"I have only one problem."

"And what's that?"

"We've been to six restaurants and I haven't had a thing to eat."

Moses slapped Clint on the back.

"That, my friend, is a problem I can easily remedy, but not at any of these places."

"Why not?"

"These are not places for the likes of you and I to eat, Clint."

"They're not?"

Moses shook his head.

"Come with me and I will take you to a place where the food will make your taste buds think they have died and gone to heaven."

TWENTY-NINE

Cinda Wolfe's inattentive blackjack player also disembarked at Natchez. He had an appointment to keep, one which he had set up with a telegraph message from Baton Rouge. As it happened his meeting was also in a restaurant, but not any of the places Clint and Moses had gone.

As the man entered Marcel's Café he looked around, searching the room with his eyes until he saw the man with the silver-tipped walking stick. He had never seen the man before, but he knew this was who he was to meet.

"Monsieur, may I get you a tab—" a waiter started to ask, but the man cut him off with a wave.

"I am meeting someone, and he already has a table."

"Of course—"

He walked away from the man and crossed the room to the table.

"Sit down," the man with the cane said, "I don't want to attract attention."

The man sat.

"Are you from Aldridge?" he asked.

The other man, who was good-looking and in his thirties, leaned forward a bit and said, "I *am* Cole Aldridge."

"Oh, Mr. Aldridge," the man said. "I didn't expect you to come yourself."

Aldridge sat back again and signaled for a waiter. When

one arrived it was the same one the first man had ignored at the door.

"Mr. Harding will have what I'm having."

Harding looked at Aldridge's plate and saw that he was eating seafood. Harding hated seafood.

"I can't eat—"

"I don't want you to eat it," Aldridge said, interrupting him, "but it would look suspicious for you to sit there with nothing in front of you."

"Oh, right. Well, since you're here I expect you got my message."

"Of course I got your message," Aldridge said. "I thought the job would be done by now, that's why I came in person. What's this complication you mentioned in your telegram?"

"Clint Adams."

Aldridge stared at Joe Harding for a few moments until Harding thought the man was going to explode. His face grew red, his eyes glazed over, and if the head on his cane had not been real silver he would have crushed it in his hand by now.

"You know him?"

"I know him."

Aldridge could not believe his luck. The last time he had crossed swords with J. P. Moses—a riverboat race between Moses's *Dead Man's Chance* and Aldridge's *Mississippi Palace*—Clint Adams had also been around. Now, when Aldridge was out for his revenge against Moses, how could Adams just happen to be in the picture again?

"You don't want to do it?" Aldridge asked.

"Oh, I'll still do it," Harding said, "but the price goes up for having to deal with the Gunsmith."

"Fine."

Emboldened, Harding said, "Double?"

"Fine," Aldridge said without hesitation. "Anything else?"

"I, uh, might need to hire more help."

"You're getting paid double now," Aldridge said. "Hire them out of your own money."

"All right, I will," Harding said, and then added, "if I need them."

The waiter returned and placed a dish in front of Harding. Looking at the food almost made him puke, and the *smell* . . .

"Anything else?" Aldridge asked.

"Oh, uh, no."

"Then get out of here before you do something disgusting."

Harding started to get up.

"And the next time you contact me," Aldridge said in a low but urgent tone, "it better be to tell me that the job is done."

"It will be," Harding said, and left.

The waiter came back as Harding was leaving.

"Your friend did not eat his dinner, monsieur."

"He's not my friend."

"Well . . . still, he did not eat. Was there anything wrong with the food?"

"No," Aldridge said, "the food is superb." In fact, he had finished his own dinner and was now eyeing the fresh plate of squid.

"But . . . it will go to waste."

"Don't worry," Aldridge said, trading the full plate for his own, "it won't."

The waiter went away and Aldridge began eating. He was one of those blessed people who could eat as much and as often as he liked without gaining weight. The walking stick was the result of a recent injury to his left foot. It had healed properly, but he had gotten used to the stick, liked it, and continued to carry it.

He thought about J. P. Moses and Clint Adams and started to be happy that Adams was in the play. He didn't dislike Adams as much as he did Moses, but it would be nice to get some revenge against both of them at the same time.

Yes, it would be *very* nice, indeed.

THIRTY

"You were right," Clint said. He sat back, rubbed his stomach, and stared across the table at Moses. "My taste buds do think they died and went to heaven."

"I told you they would," Moses said with great satisfaction. "I've tried for years to get Antoine to come to work for me, to cook on my boat, but he doesn't want to give up his restaurant."

Clint looked around the place, which was appropriately called Antoine's. He could see why the man wouldn't want to give it up. Every table in the place was filled.

"How about some coffee?" Moses asked.

"Always."

"You'll like Antoine's coffee," Moses said, "I guarantee it."

"Well, you were right about the food," Clint said, "so I'm not about to argue with you."

Moses called the waiter over and ordered the coffee, then sat back and looked at Clint.

"You look like you've got something on your mind."

"I guess I do."

"Spit it out."

"I've been thinking about Masters."

"What about him?"

"We've docked in Baton Rouge and Concordia," Clint said, "and now here."

"And you're wondering why he hasn't tried something, right?"

"Right."

Moses shrugged.

"Maybe he's given up."

"Those attempts in Biloxi were too serious," Clint said. "I don't think he's just going to give up and forget about it, Jack."

"Well, I didn't think so, either," Moses said, "but maybe we're both wrong about Captain Masters. Maybe he got himself another boat and he's too busy to bother with us anymore."

"I'd like to believe that," Clint said, "but I just can't."

"No," Moses said, "neither do I, but there's no use in wondering, Clint. When he does try something else we just have to be ready for it."

"Ever vigilant," Clint said, "that's us."

The waiter came with the coffee, and they waited while he poured and then left the pot.

"That's the blackest coffee I ever saw," Clint said.

"And it'll take the lining off your stomach," Moses said. "It's great!"

Clint tasted it, put his cup down, and said, "Whew! You're right."

"It's good."

"It's taking the lining off my stomach right now," Clint said. "I can feel it."

"See?" Moses said. "I told you. It's good."

THIRTY-ONE

When Clint and Moses left Antoine's, Clint thought he could still feel the coffee tearing layers from his stomach. He didn't think he'd ever find coffee that was too strong for him, but it had happened at Antoine's.

"It's getting dark," Moses said. "I want to get back before the girls arrive. I don't want Laura to get ahold of them. She might convert them."

"What's going on with Laura?" Clint asked.

"What do you mean?"

"Well, it's obvious you're not seeing her anymore."

"I never said I'd continue to see her," Moses said. "She knew that. So did you."

"So who are you seeing now?"

"I'm not seeing any one woman now," Moses said. "Why? Has Laura complained to you?"

"No, she hasn't."

"And she won't," Moses said. "She likes her job and she's doing it well."

"Does that mean you'd fire her if she started to complain?"

"No," Moses said, "it means I can trust her to be professional."

"Well, then—"

Clint stopped short as they passed an alley. It was nothing he heard or saw, but rather something he *felt*.

"Wha—" Moses started to say, but Clint pushed him and shouted, "Down!" just as there was a shot.

Clint felt a burning pain in his left shoulder as he threw himself to the ground and rolled. He came up with his gun in his hand, as did Moses, and they both looked around for the source of the shot.

"Where?" Moses shouted.

"I'm not sure," Clint said. "I'll look high, you look low."

They got to their feet and started looking. Clint was studying the second- and third-story rooms, as well as the rooftops. Moses was looking at ground level, alleys, windows, doorways. Neither of them was seeing anything or anyone, and there were no further shots.

"Were they after me or you?" Moses asked.

"I don't know who they were after," Clint said, looking at his shoulder, "but they got me."

"How bad?" Moses asked with concern.

"More damage to my jacket than me."

"Let's get you to a doctor."

"Let's get back to the boat before someone tries again," Clint said.

"Are you sure—"

"I'm fine, Jack," Clint said. "Let's get off the street."

"All right," Moses said, "but I'll keep looking low and you keep looking high."

"Deal."

THIRTY-TWO

They got back to the *Biloxi Queen* without further incident.

"I'll have one of the women look at my shoulder," Clint said.

"Go to your cabin," Moses said. "I'll have Mr. Bixby come down. He's good with wounds."

"All right. You'd better check and see if your girls are here."

"I will," Moses said, "but I want to put my men on alert. I don't want to get boarded again. Isn't it funny how we were just wondering when Captain Masters was going to rear his ugly head again?"

"You think it was Masters?"

"Who else?"

"Then you think he was after you."

Moses shrugged.

"If you hadn't shoved me maybe I would have taken the bullet instead of you. By the way, thanks for shoving me."

"Don't mention it."

"I'll see you in your cabin."

"Right."

When there was a knock at his cabin door, Clint palmed his gun and called out, "Come."

The door opened and Bixby came in, carrying some instruments and gauze. Behind him came Cinda Wolfe, carrying a basin of water.

"What are you doing here?" Clint asked her.

"I heard what happened," she said. "I wanted to make sure you were all right."

"I'm fine."

He had taken off his jacket and shirt by the time they arrived.

"I just wanted to . . . help."

"You can help by putting that basin down so I can use it," Bixby said.

She put it down on a table next to the bed. Bixby began to clean the wounds while Cinda watched.

"Just creased you," Bixby said. "Either somebody was a bad shot or you were a moving target."

"I was moving."

"Smart man. Who shot you?"

"We don't know."

"Was he after you or Mr. Moses?"

"We don't know that either."

"Well, I guess you know enough to watch your step from now on."

"I always watch my step," Clint said. "That's why one of us isn't dead."

"Mr. Moses said you pushed him out of the way before the shot. How did you know someone was going to shoot at you?"

"I don't know, Cinda," Clint said.

"You didn't see or hear anything that warned you?"

"No."

"Then how—"

"Sometimes I just know when something is going to

happen,'' Clint said. ''It's like an extra sense I've developed over the years.''

''From having people shoot at you a lot, you mean?''

''Yes.''

''How many times have you been shot, Clint?''

''I don't know,'' he said.

''You don't *know*?'' She was incredulous. ''How can you not know how many times—has it been *that* many?''

''I haven't kept count, Cinda.''

''I don't—I can't believe—I have to go.''

She went out the door in a hurry.

''What's wrong with her?'' Clint asked.

''She's a woman,'' Bixby said, tying the bandage on Clint's shoulder tight.

''Ow! I know she's a woman—''

''They don't understand about things like gettin' shot and bein' stabbed.''

Clint looked at Bixby.

''How many times have you been shot?''

''None.''

''Stabbed?''

''I been stabbed.''

''How many times?''

Bixby stood up and picked up the basin, which was now filled with bloody water.

''Like you, I don't stop to keep count. I don't think that'll get infected, but I can check it in a day or two.''

''Thanks, Mr. Bixby.''

''Sure. Thanks for keeping the boss from gettin' killed. Don't know what would happen to my job if that happened.''

''Don't mention it.''

Bixby started for the door, then turned and said, ''Not

that that's the only reason I'm glad he's not dead, ya understand.''

"I understand, Mr. Bixby."

"Good. Don't be swinging that arm around for a while."

"I won't."

"That ain't your gun arm, is it?"

"No."

"Well," Bixby said, "that's good."

Actually, even if it had been his gun arm Clint didn't think the wound would have impeded him much. It didn't even hurt all that much, at the moment.

He donned a clean shirt, wondering if he should go and talk to Cinda. No, maybe not. Whatever was bothering her, she was going to have to work it out for herself.

He left the cabin and went to find Moses.

THIRTY-THREE

"I heard you got shot."

Clint was standing on the deck, looking down at the dock. Moses had set up a watch for his men, and Clint had decided to deal himself in and take one. He was on duty from midnight to two a.m.

He turned and saw Darla standing there. She was not wearing her working clothes.

"Quit early tonight?"

She shrugged.

"Men don't seem as interested when we're docked," she said. "It's not something I can explain. How about you?"

It was his turn to shrug.

"I'm surprised any man wouldn't be interested in you, no matter where they were or what they were doing."

"You're not."

"I'm on watch, Darla."

"Why?"

"You said you'd heard about me getting shot."

"I also heard you were all right," she said, "and that you weren't sure who they were shooting at, you or Mr. Moses."

"That's all true."

"Why are you on watch, then? Why not his men?"

"They are," he said. "I decided to help out."

"Cinda's real upset, you know."

"Is she?"

They remained silent for a few moments.

"What did she say?" he asked.

"Nothing, to me," Darla said. "She's too much of a princess to talk to the likes of me. I heard her talking to Laura, though. Something about not understanding how you could not know how many times you been shot."

"That's so . . ."

"Ridiculous?"

"Yes."

"I agree," Darla said. "Don't she know men shoot each other and get shot? It's what they do."

"Maybe not where she came from."

"Where's that?"

"You know," he said after a moment, "I don't know."

"Probably the East," Darla said. "They don't shoot each other as much in the East, do they?"

"Not as much, no," Clint said, "but they do it."

"So what are you on watch for?"

"Somebody boarding the boat."

"Don't think they'll do that."

"Why not?"

"Whoever shot you did it from hiding, right?"

"That's right."

"Man like that wouldn't try to come onboard," she said, "not with all of Mr. Moses's men here. I think you're safe."

He didn't bother telling her about the boarding in Biloxi. She did have a point, though. They did have less men on-board then.

"How long you on watch for?"

"Until two.""

"I'll still be up then."

He looked at her.

"You know," she said, "if you wanted to talk . . . or somethin'."

They looked at each other for a few more moments.

"Well, thanks, Darla," he said finally. "I'll keep that in mind."

"You know where my cabin is?"

"Yes."

He knew where all the girls' cabins were, as well as some of the crew.

"Glad to hear it."

She had been standing with her arms folded the entire time. Now she turned away, dropping them to her sides. He watched as she walked to a gangway that would take her down a level. She stopped there and turned, caught him watching. Since he *was* caught, he didn't bother trying to pretend he wasn't.

"If I was sharing a man's bed," she said, "I'd sure be able to tell *him* how many times he been shot."

She went down, leaving him wondering about her method.

THIRTY-FOUR

At two a.m. Moses came out himself to relieve Clint.

"Nothing moving down there," Clint said.

"I don't expect there to be," Moses said, leaning on the railing. "Not really."

"Why not?" Clint asked. He wanted to hear if Moses's logic was the same as Darla's—and it was.

"Somebody who tries to shoot from ambush is not going to try any sort of a frontal assault."

"I don't think that boarding the *Queen* at night would exactly be called a frontal assault, Jack, but basically I agree with you."

"We'll keep the watch on, though," Moses said. "Just to be on the safe side. Too many innocent people are aboard."

Clint nodded his agreement.

"You might as well go and get some sleep."

"All right."

"Oh, one thing."

"What's that?"

"A couple of players came onboard today," Moses said. "I think I can get you a decent game now, starting tomorrow night."

"Good," Clint said. "I'll look forward to it."

"Good night, Clint."

Clint waved and went down below, where he and the crew had cabins. He had insisted to Moses that he not be given a guest cabin, but the same one the crew used. That way, he said, Moses could get money for the better one. That was an argument J. P. Moses chose not to argue with.

It happened almost without his consent. One minute he was walking to his own cabin and the next he was standing in front of Darla's. He almost knocked, but decided not to. It was so quiet someone might hear it. He decided to leave it up to fate. If she was expecting him, the door would be unlocked. If it wasn't, then he'd go to his own cabin.

He tried the door, found it unlocked, opened it, and stepped inside. She had kept a lamp lit down low, so that the room was bathed in a soft glow. He closed the door quietly behind him.

"I'm not asleep," she said from the bed. "You don't have to be quiet."

"I didn't think you were asleep," he said. "That's not why I'm being quiet."

"Oh."

She sat up in bed, allowing the sheet to fall away from her. She was naked, so there was no mistake why she had left the door unlocked. Her breasts were large and firm, with very dark nipples. The room smelled of her—not of her perfume, but of *her*.

"Did you come to . . . talk?"

"Sure," Clint said, approaching the bed, "we'll talk . . . too."

He sat next to her and studied her skin. It was so smooth, so dark. He reached out and touched her with his fingertips. He felt her shoulders, her neck, then the slopes of her breasts. She closed her eyes and touched the tip of her tongue to her full lower lip as his fingertips brushed her nipples.

He leaned in and kissed her mouth, softly at first, and then more urgently as she pressed her lips tightly to his. She moaned and opened her mouth, and their tongues danced and then entwined.

She began to pull at his clothing, and together they peeled it from him. She kissed his chest, running her tongue around his nipples, sliding her hand down into his lap. She stroked him, gently at first, and then began to tug on him as she continued to kiss his chest, his shoulders, his neck, and then his mouth again. She had the softest mouth he'd ever felt, and he found that he couldn't get enough of it.

He put his arms around her then and pulled her to him. Their bodies pressed together, her breasts flattening against his chest, her skin hot against his. He moved onto the bed with her, sitting across from her, and they slid their legs over each other's so they could move closer. His rigid penis was pressed against her wet vagina, and they kissed that way for a while.

She rubbed up against him like a cat, moaning as she became wetter still. Finally she leaned, hands pressed to the mattress, taking her weight on her arms. She lifted her butt up and then slid down on him, taking him inside her. He reached for her and gathered her in until she was sitting in his lap, with his cock buried deep inside of her.

"Oooh, yeah, baby," she crooned as they began to move, "oh, God, yes . . ." She began to bounce up and down on his lap, up and down, sliding up on him and then coming down hard, driving him deeply inside of her, forcing grunts and groans of pleasure from both of them.

For a moment Clint wondered if anyone could hear them, but then he forgot about that. Her breasts were rubbing against his chest, her nipples hardened, like pebbles, as she continued to bounce on him. He knew that if he allowed her to continue this way he wasn't going to last long, so he made a move.

He rocked forward, forcing her to climb off of him. He pressed her down onto the bed and got to his knees over her. He began to kiss her, pushing his hand down between her legs to feel her wetness.

"Oooh, God," she said, "you're touching me . . . oooh, *there*, right there! That's . . . that's it . . ."

He watched her face as he continued to use his fingers on her. He liked the way her eyes widened, as if in shock, the way her nostrils flared, and the way she bit her lips. She moved her butt, rubbing it against the sheet, then pushing her crotch up against his hand.

"No man's ever . . . done that before . . ." she gasped.

"There's more," he whispered, kissing her chin and then her lush mouth, "much more. I want to know every inch of you."

"Oh, baby," she said, her eyes widening again, "and I want to be known!"

THIRTY-FIVE

Clint took his time and did exactly what he said he would do. He got to know Darla intimately, using his mouth and hands. He'd found himself doing this with most of the women he'd been with lately. In fact, he'd done it with Cinda.

Thinking of Cinda gave him a brief moment of guilt, but they had not pledged themselves to each other. Even she had made that clear. Also, she'd made it pretty clear that she didn't want to be with him tonight. She was still trying to deal with the fact that he didn't keep count of the number of times he'd been shot.

After he had been all over Darla with his mouth, he settled down between her beautiful thighs.

"What are you—oooh, oooh, you . . . you beautiful man!"

He licked her, and licked her, and licked her until she couldn't take it anymore.

"Stop, stop," she said, beating on him with one fist.

"Hey!" he said, looking up at her.

She was panting as she pushed the words out.

"My . . . turn . . . my turn . . . lie down . . ."

Why not? he thought. If she wanted to take a turn at him, he was only too happy to allow her to.

He lay down on his back and she began to explore him,

129

using those soft, cushy lips and her long, graceful fingers. When she finally centered on his penis, he moaned and lifted his butt off the bed.

She slid her lips down over him and slowly took all of him into her mouth. She began to suck him wetly, riding him up and down with her mouth, using her fingers as well so that she was both sucking him and stroking him. The combination was hard to fight, and before he could push her away he suddenly erupted. As he ejaculated it felt like a geyser and he cried out in pleasure. She continued to suck on him until he had no more to give and then she released him. She seemed surprised that he was still hard—and so was he.

"Oh, my," she said, and with a smile she mounted him and slid him inside of her.

"I don't think—" he started, but she put one hand over his mouth.

"I *do* think," she said, and started riding him.

Her breasts swayed before his eyes, and he lifted his head and took them in his hands, licking and sucking her nipples. She pressed her hands down on his belly, bracing herself, lifting up and coming down on him as hard as she could, grunting with the effort.

Because he had ejaculated already he lasted longer than either of them had expected, to the delight of both of them.

"God," she said at one point, "I think you're going to stay hard all *night*."

It wasn't quite all night, but Darla seemed intent on riding him as long as he *was* hard. He felt her body quiver and react to her pleasure several times before he finally exploded again, and this time it just sort of made things go black—either that or the lamp had gone out.

•   •   •

"When the lamp went out," she said later, "I thought I went blind."

"I know," he said, tightening his arms around her, "I thought I was blind, too."

"God," she said, laughing, "imagine if we had screwed each other blind?"

"They'd find us in the morning, bumping into each other. . . ." he said.

She pressed herself against him, slid her hand down between his legs, and said, "They might find us doing that, anyway."

Amazingly, he felt himself reacting to her touch, starting to harden again.

"You don't get enough, do you?" she asked.

"Not enough of you, I guess."

"You're gonna make me sore," she said, sliding one leg over him. "I won't be able to work."

"Mmmm," he said, as he slid right into her wetness, "try explaining that to Laura."

Still later she said, "They all want you, you know."

"Who does?"

"All the women onboard."

"That's silly," he said. "They can't all want me."

"They're all curious, then."

"About what?"

"About your legend."

He laughed.

"My legend."

"Like it or not, you are a legend."

"What legend are we talking about?"

"Well . . . there's talk you've been with a lot of women."

"Oh," he said, "that legend."

They both laughed.

"Can I ask you a question?" she said.

"Sure."

"Did you think of Cinda . . . once?"

He decided to tell the truth.

"One time."

"Guilty?"

"For about a minute."

She squeezed him and said, "I'm glad you told me the truth."

They lay together in silence for a few minutes.

"Do you think she's waiting in your room?"

"Jesus," he said, "I hope not."

"I don't think so," she said. "She was pretty . . . confused before. I guess confused is the word."

"She'll have to figure it out for herself."

"She's all grown up," Darla agreed.

"Right."

"No need for anyone to feel guilty."

"Right."

"We're *all* grown up."

"That we are."

After a moment she asked, "Is it all right if I feel a little smug?"

He slapped her on the butt—which, curiously, got them started all over again.

"Clint?"

"Hmm?"

"Are you asleep yet?"

"Almost."

Her fingers sought out a scar on his body in the dark, a

puckered one, and she said, "I can tell you how many times you been shot, if you want me to."

"To tell you the truth," he said, "I'd rather just go to sleep."

She kissed the scar—she knew how many he had, because she'd counted them all with her mouth—and said, "Good night."

THIRTY-SIX

When Clint woke the next morning Darla was on the other side of the bed, curled up so that her rounded butt was to him. He gave a moment's thought to waking her, but he seriously didn't think he'd be able to handle her again. He'd had sex with her more times that night than he'd ever had with another woman before. Toward the end, especially the last time, it started to become painful—although it was a *good* kind of pain.

He slid from the bed easily, so as not to wake her, and got dressed. As he reached the door, though, she spoke.

"I'm glad you didn't try anything," she said. "To tell you the truth, I don't think I would be able to handle you again. I'm so *tired*."

"I'll see you later."

"Don't you come over here and touch me or kiss me," she warned, "or we gonna find out if we can screw each other to death."

"Why don't we save that for another time, Darla?" he suggested.

"Mmmm," she said, and started to snore lightly.

Could it be done? he wondered.

He shook his head and left the cabin.

• • •

He went back to his cabin for some fresh clothes. He opened the door slowly, hoping that he wouldn't find Cinda waiting in his bed. To his relief, his bed was as he had left it, and had not been slept in. He closed the door, found his fresh clothes, set them aside, and used the pitcher and basin to wash up.

He hoped that nothing had happened during the night. He suspected that as occupied as he and Darla were with each other they probably wouldn't have heard a thing.

He finished washing, put on his clean clothes, and went to get some breakfast.

He was *sore*, but he was still hungry.

When he got to the main dining room it was nine a.m., and he found Moses already there.

"You look beat," Moses said.

"I'm fine."

Moses was already working on a breakfast of ham, eggs, potatoes, and biscuits.

"Have some coffee," he said to Clint, "yours will be out in a minute."

"How'd you know I'd be here at this time?"

"Educated guess," Moses said. "I have the feeling you didn't spend the night in your own cabin."

"Whose was I in?"

Moses gave him a long stare.

"The two of you were making a lot of noise when I went by."

"Oh."

There were a few moments of silence and then Moses said, "Don't be asking me about Laura anymore. That would be the pot calling the kettle black, now wouldn't it?"

Clint turned away from Moses's look and said, "Where's my breakfast?"

Over breakfast they discussed how the all-night watch went.

"Nobody saw a thing," Moses said. "I checked first thing this morning."

"When do we leave?" Clint asked.

"Noon."

"Why not earlier?"

"Because we'll be taking on more passengers this morning. Remember, I'm in this to make money."

"I remember. Did the girls all get on all right? I meant to ask last night."

"All right and on time."

"You know, they're going to need dresses."

"I've got dresses onboard," Moses said, "all sizes and shapes."

"You do plan ahead, don't you?"

"I try to."

"Speaking of planning ahead," Clint said, "are you planning on arming your men?"

"No."

"Why not?"

"A couple of reasons. One, I don't think anyone is going to try anything while we're out on the river, and two, half of them would probably shoot a toe off, and blow a hole in my boat at the same time."

"Well," Clint said, "I really like that last reason. I'd call that good thinking."

"Thanks."

"They could even shoot one of us by accident."

Moses frowned.

"I hadn't thought of that. I guess it *was* a good idea not to arm them."

"Better than you thought," Clint said. "It's bad enough being shot at from ambush—that *really* makes me mad—but being shot by accident would be even worse."

"When you get right down to it," Moses said, "being shot is being shot. You're just as dead."

"Let's just work on not getting shot at all," Clint said.

"Agreed."

THIRTY-SEVEN

Their next stop after Natchez was Vicksburg. After that Moses said they weren't going to stop until they reached Memphis. That night Clint sat in on his first poker game of the trip, and Moses was there at the start to make the introductions.

There were five players and Clint was the last to arrive at the table. He'd been waiting at the bar, nursing a beer, watching the other players arrive.

"Do you know any of them?" Eric asked from behind the bar.

"No," Clint said, "not that I can remember."

"You remember everyone you've ever played cards with?" he asked, looking surprised.

"No," Clint said patiently, "I don't, that's why I said—never mind."

"Are you waiting to go over last?"

"Yes."

"Why?"

"I just want to get a look at the players before I sit down."

At that point Moses came over and said, "Everybody else is there."

"Do you know these players?"

"One or two," Moses said. "The others just flashed enough cash at me to get into the game."

"No references?"

"I'm trying to make some money here, Clint."

"In a private game?"

"If they have a good game they'll send others to play at my tables," Moses said. "So do me a favor, give them a good game."

"Do you want me to let them win?"

"No," Moses said, "but carry them awhile before you take all their money."

"Sure," Clint said, putting his beer mug down, "fine."

"You want a fresh beer for the game?" Eric asked.

"No," Clint said, "I don't drink when I'm playing poker." He looked at Moses and said, "Let's go."

"Clint Adams," Moses said, "meet Steven Womack, Bruce Stilwell, Gar Anthony, Bill Palmer, and Tom Ross."

Clint nodded to each man in turn. Womack and Anthony were about his age, Palmer and Ross were younger. Stilwell's age was hard to tell. If you were to judge them by appearance, Womack, Anthony, and Palmer were dressed in dark suits, a look gamblers usually favored. Stilwell had a suit on, but it was light-colored. Tom Ross was dressed in jeans and a work shirt, and was wearing a holstered gun. If the others were armed their weapons were out of sight.

"Gentlemen," Clint said.

"Let's discuss the conditions," Moses said. "Would you gentlemen prefer to deal your own games, or shall I provide a dealer?"

"Since we're not familiar with each other," Bruce Stilwell offered, "I would suggest that we allow Mr. Moses to supply a dealer."

"Any arguments?" Moses asked.

He looked around and no one offered one.

"Fine," Moses said, and waved his hand. He'd had a dealer standing by in anticipation of the players' request.

"This is Danny," Moses said. "He's a very experienced dealer."

Danny was in his forties. He was trim in a white shirt and black trousers.

"Gentlemen," he said.

There were several sealed decks of cards in the center of the table.

Moses went over the rules of the game very quickly. There were no limits on betting except for a minimum, or on raising. The game they all chose was seven-card stud. It would remain so until other players joined the game, in which case it would become five-card stud.

"And now," Moses said, "chips."

He waved and two men came over carrying chips. They proceeded to accept cash from the players, the ones who were not being extended credit by Moses. Clint noticed that he and Ross were the only two who weren't dealing in cash. He assumed that Ross was one of the players Moses knew personally.

Clint studied Tom Ross. He decided that the man was not as young as he appeared. His hands, as he stacked his chips, looked like they belonged to someone who had done a lot of work over the years, and yet his face was seamless. He decided that the man could pass for forty, but was probably ten years older than that.

Each player started with five hundred dollars. Clint was not a rich man, but he did little else with his money so that he would be able to play in games like this when the opportunity arose.

They received four different colored chips, and each player stacked them to his liking.

"When you gentlemen are ready," Moses said, "just let your dealer know, and good luck."

As Moses walked away the dealer asked, "May I break the seal?"

"We aren't going to get a chance to play if you don't," Gar Anthony said. Anthony seemed to have an attitude already. Clint decided to keep an eye on him.

Actually, for the first hour of the game he'd be keeping an eye on everyone. He knew a professional gambler who once told him he never won a hand the first hour because he was busy watching the players. Clint didn't go that far. He didn't want to pass up a good hand if one came along, but he folded a lot more hands than he played during the first hour of any poker game he got into.

He watched as the dealer chose a deck and set the others aside. He cracked the seal and began to expertly shuffle the cards.

"Gentlemen," he said, when he had them mixed to his own satisfaction, "let's play poker."

THIRTY-EIGHT

It didn't take Clint an hour to pick out the dangerous player. It was Tom Ross who, from appearances, would seem to be the least likely candidate.

Womack, Anthony, and Palmer dressed like gamblers, but they didn't play that way. None of the three men seemed to know when to stay in and when to go out. Consequently, they stayed in a lot of hands much too long. As for Stilwell, he seemed to know what he was doing, he just didn't seem to have much playing luck.

Having three people in the game who didn't know when to fold made it very difficult for Clint, Ross, and Stilwell to play the game properly. Of course, once Clint figured out that the three men stayed in too often he was able to use that information. He assumed that Stilwell and Ross would do the same.

One hand in particular was very indicative of the way the game was going. It took place midway through the second hour of the game.

The opening bet of the game fell to Clint, whose first card was an ace. Ross also drew an ace, but since Clint had gotten his first it was his bet.

Since he also had an ace in the hole he bet twenty dollars on his pair of aces—although, more often than not, it had been his experience that being dealt two aces in the first three cards was almost the kiss of death.

The players called his bet in turn: Stilwell, Palmer, Womack, Anthony, and then Ross.

The dealer dealt the second card.

Clint caught a king. He had a king in the hole, so he now had aces and kings.

Stilwell was showing a pair of deuces.

Palmer had a queen of hearts and a ten of spades showing.

Womack had a pair of eights.

Anthony had two cards which were about as far apart as they could get, a deuce of clubs and a jack of hearts.

Ross got a jack to go with his ace.

"Fifty dollars," Clint said, to force someone out of the pot.

"Call," Stilwell said. Of course he'd see the bet, he had a pair.

Palmer had a queen and a ten, so it was possible he could have made a straight. However, he folded.

Womack called with his pair.

When it came Anthony's turn Clint would have expected anyone else to fold. He had a deuce, and there were two others on the table, and he had a jack, with another one showing on the table. Unless he had very good cards underneath, he should have folded. However, he called the bet.

Ross called the bet.

As far as Clint was concerned Anthony should have folded immediately and Palmer should have called, yet the two men did the opposite. One didn't know when to go out, and the other didn't know when to stay in.

Of course, it was possible that Anthony could have had good hole cards, but Clint doubted it.

When the fifth card was drawn Clint still had two pair, Stilwell still had one pair, as did Womack. Anthony did not improve at all, nor did Ross, but he had three high cards on the table to a straight, a ten, a jack, and an ace. Perhaps he had the other ace in the hole, but it was more likely he was going for the straight, if he didn't already have it.

"A hundred dollars," Clint said. That would surely drive Anthony from the game.

Stilwell considered his pair of deuces and looked across the table at the deuce in Anthony's hand.

"Fold."

It was a sound move.

Womack called with his pair. Maybe he had two pair also, or possibly three of a kind. However, Clint felt sure the man would have raised if he had three of a kind.

"I call," Anthony said, and all the men at the table looked at him.

"What?" he asked, but no one answered. It seemed clear to everyone in the game that he should have folded.

"I raise a hundred," Ross said.

Clint felt sure he had his straight, but he had to call because another king or ace would give him a full house.

"Call."

"Call," Womack said.

They all looked at Anthony, who had absolutely nothing on the table.

"I call."

With a more knowledgeable player Clint might have thought that the man had something good in the hole, possibly a pair that matched one of his cards on the table.

However, he felt that Anthony simply didn't know what the proper play was in this situation.

"Sixth card," the dealer said.

Clint got a deuce, the last of the twos. Now the one Anthony had was worth nothing.

If Ross had a straight he had the strong hand, but Clint didn't want the man to know that. He wanted Ross to think that he could beat a straight.

"A hundred."

Womack looked at his pair of eights. Across the table from him Ross had drawn an eight. Clint was betting into Ross's raise, and Womack assumed Ross was going to raise again.

"I'm out." He had nothing else in the hole, and even if he caught the third eight, Clint or Ross would probably beat him. It was the proper play, which surprised Clint. Perhaps the man was not as bad a player as he'd first appeared.

Anthony, however, continued to puzzle everyone. His table cards were now a deuce—and a *dead* deuce at that—a jack of hearts, and he'd just drawn a five of clubs. In fact, he shocked everyone by raising.

"I raise a hundred."

Clint and Ross exchanged a glance.

"Raise another hundred," Ross said.

Clint still had two chances at a king and one chance for an ace, three chances to fill his hand.

"Two hundred to you, Mr. Adams," the dealer said.

"Call the two hundred."

Stilwell, Palmer, Womack had folded.

"A hundred to you, Mr. Anthony."

Anthony responded without a thought.

"I call the hundred."

"Last card," the dealer said, dealing it facedown.

Clint looked at his last card and made his bet.

"Two hundred."

Anthony looked around the table, a trapped look on his face. He had stayed in this long and Clint could tell that pride was going to cost him money. The man was afraid he'd lose face if he folded now.

"C-call."

"Mr. Ross?" the dealer said.

"I'll just call," Ross said. "I don't think my straight is going to beat Mr. Adams's full house."

"You're called, Mr. Adams," Danny, the dealer, said.

"Full house," Clint said, turning his cards over, "kings over aces."

"Damn!" Anthony said. He threw his cards down face-up, revealing that he had jacks and fives. With two pair he never should have been in the hand.

"How did you know he had a full house?" Anthony asked Ross.

Ross folded his cards without revealing them, although Clint was sure the man had had an ace high straight—amazing, considering the amount of picture cards that had been on the table. He had been lucky enough to fill the hand, but unlucky enough to fill it at the wrong time.

"Experience, Mr. Anthony," Ross said.

"With two pair you never should have been in that hand," Stilwell said. "Hell, I folded queens over."

"You had queens over deuces and you folded?" Anthony asked. "Why?"

"If you were watching," Stilwell said, as Clint raked in his chips, "you saw that all the deuces were out, and one queen was out. I was not willing to pay to go fishing for that last queen."

Anthony stared at him.

"The deuces were out?"

"Next hand, dealer," Ross said, stacking his chips. "We're here to play poker, not teach it."

"What are you tryin' to say?" Anthony demanded.

"Just that it will be very expensive for you to learn poker at this table, Mr. Anthony."

"I know how to play poker," Anthony replied. "Besides, I've got the money to lose, if I want to."

Clint doubted that the man knew what he was saying. Nobody plays poker figuring they have the money to lose.

That is, unless they've got a *lot* of money.

THIRTY-NINE

That was the way the game went most of the night, with Gar Anthony losing heavily and becoming more and more angry. He wasn't angry about losing money, though. The money had little to do with it. It was his pride that was hurt. Wild Bill Hickok had always told Clint that a prideful man shouldn't gamble, he had too much to lose.

Joe Harding watched Clint Adams play poker from across the room. He had decided that he was losing too much money trying to keep an eye on Moses and Adams while playing blackjack. Also, the dealer's breasts were a distraction.

Harding was upset with himself. He'd almost managed to get rid of Clint Adams in Natchez. Spotting Moses and Adams on the street was a stroke of luck. He'd quickly purchased a rifle and gotten himself to a rooftop. From there he could have picked either one of them off, but he thought it would be fitting to take care of the Gunsmith on land, and J. P. Moses on the water.

How Clint Adams had reacted that quickly was beyond him. It was almost as if the man had moved even before he triggered his rifle.

He'd left the rifle on the roof after one shot and gotten

away from there. With a man like Clint Adams you didn't try a second shot.

After his failure he had gotten to a telegraph office and sent a message to some men he knew. They were going to meet him in Memphis. He had until they reached there to decide if he wanted them to board, or if they would simply take care of both Moses and Adams when they disembarked.

Both men had left the boat at every port, so Harding decided to play this as if they would do the same when they reached Memphis.

There was a lot of money riding on this and he'd already been careless once. He hadn't *really* been careless, but he decided not to take any more chances, especially not with Clint Adams. The man seemed to have an extra sense, which was probably why he was alive after all these years. But he wasn't in some dusty cow town, and he wasn't on a horse, he was in Joe Harding's backyard.

Memphis would be the last place he'd ever see.

He was as good as dead.

By the end of the night Clint was the furthest ahead with Ross right behind him. Stilwell had held about even, Womack and Palmer had lost considerably, but Gar Anthony had lost *very* heavily.

"We can't stop now," Anthony complained, "I was gettin' hot."

To make matters worse, about halfway through the game—after losing a particularly brutal hand where he'd actually had good cards and *still* lost—Anthony had started drinking whiskey.

Clint looked around and saw that all of the action except for their table had ceased for the night. In fact, it wasn't night, it was morning, and very nearly daylight.

As if he had some sort of sixth sense that the game was over, J. P. Moses appeared at that moment to cash them out.

"Are you fellas about to call it a night?"

"We *are* calling it a night, Mr. Moses," the dealer said. "All the players agree, except for Mr. Anthony here."

"Was gettin' hot, I was," Anthony complained. His eyes could barely focus.

"Maybe you'll have better luck tonight, Mr. Anthony," Moses said. "The gaming room is closed for the night."

"Bad luck," Anthony muttered, " 's all it was, bad luck . . ."

He started to get up, then fell back down in his chair, barely conscious.

"Danny," Moses instructed, "get someone to help you take Mr. Anthony to his cabin."

"We can help," Stilwell said. "Mr. Ross?"

"Not me," Ross said. "Cash me out, please?"

Moses redeemed Ross's chips and then the man left the room.

"I'll help," Womack said.

"Thank you, gentlemen," Danny said.

In the end it was Danny, Womack, Stilwell, *and* Palmer who helped Anthony from the table and to his cabin. Moses assured them they could hold on to their chips and either use them again or redeem them later.

"How did you do?" Moses asked.

"I did well," Clint said.

"Coffee?"

"Sure."

"Bring your chips to the bar," Moses said, "and I'll cash you out there."

As they reached the bar, Moses said, "Eric, coffee."

"Comin' up."

Eric poured out two cups while Moses counted Clint's chips and then handed him his cash.

"You weren't kidding," Moses said. "You did *extremely* well."

"Most of it belonged to Gar Anthony," Clint said. "I thought you said these were good players. Anthony is possibly the worst player I've ever seen, and Womack and Palmer don't really know what to do when they get deep into a hand."

"I didn't say they were all good players," Moses said, "I said they could all afford to play. There's a difference."

"That's what Anthony was saying," Clint said, "that he could afford to lose."

"There you go."

"He can afford the money, Jack, but his pride can't take it."

"Hickok used to say—"

Clint cut him off before he could continue.

"I know," Clint said, "I remember."

"You want me to ban him from the game?"

"Hell, no," Clint said. "Let anyone who can afford to play go ahead and sit in."

"Will you play against him again?"

"I hate to take his money," Clint said, then grinned and said, "but I'll force myself."

"I thought you might."

"Just have someone keep an eye out for trouble from him," Clint said. "Nobody's pride can take *that* much punishment."

"Don't worry, I'll take care of it," Moses promised.

FORTY

When Clint got to his room he was glad to find it empty. He didn't think he had the energy to deal with a woman, whether it was Cinda or Darla. He removed his clothes, dropped them on the floor, and fell onto the bed. He was asleep in minutes.

When he woke up he checked the time and saw that he had been asleep for five hours. He actually felt as if it had been longer than that, he was so refreshed. He got up, washed himself, and dressed in fresh clothes. He left the dirty clothes in a pile—as Moses had people onboard who would wash them for him, and the crew—and went up on deck.

He walked around the deck for a while before going up to the wheelhouse. There he found the captain, Mr. Bixby, and J. P. Moses.

"Come on in, Clint," Moses said, opening the door of the wheelhouse for him.

"What's going on?" Clint asked. "A meeting of the minds?"

"No," Moses said, "I just like it up here."

"How's the shoulder?" Bixby asked.

"It's fine, thanks to you."

"Not me," Bixby said, shaking his head, "it just wasn't that bad a wound."

"Thanks just the same."

Bixby nodded, accepting the thanks.

Clint looked out the window at the muddy Mississippi speeding by.

"We're going pretty fast," he commented.

"We're making good time," Moses said. "I just came up to see if we could let her out and see what she can do."

"We're clear for a while," the captain said. "We can run 'er."

"How does she compare with the *Chance*?" Clint asked Moses.

The man smiled at the mention of his other boat.

"She doesn't," he said. "There's not a boat on the Mississippi that can compare with the *Chance*. You were here when we proved that."

"That was when we raced Aldridge's boat . . . what was it called?"

"The *Mississippi Palace*," Moses said.

"Whatever happened to Aldridge?"

"He's still around," Moses said, "still doing business up and down the river."

"On the river?"

"No," Moses said, "he's stayed off the river since the *Dead Man's Chance* beat his boat."

"What about him?" Clint asked.

"What about him?" Moses replied, looking puzzled.

"What if he was behind that bushwhacking and not Masters?"

"Why?"

Clint shrugged.

"Maybe he still holds a grudge against you."

"And you?"

"Maybe."

Moses thought awhile, rubbing his jaw, then shook his head.

"It's got to be Masters," Moses said. "It's just too much of a coincidence—I mean, we *know* Masters was behind that stuff in Biloxi."

"I know I hate coincidence," Clint said, "but Masters sent some hard cases after us. This time someone tried to shoot one of us in the back. He got one shot off and disappeared. He would have gotten away with it if I hadn't sensed something."

"You think he was a professional?" Moses asked. "A hired killer?"

"It's possible."

"If that's the case," Moses said, "then he'll probably try again, maybe in Memphis."

"How would he know that we're stopping in Memphis?" Clint asked.

"Most boats stop in Memphis."

"Yeah, but how would he know when we got there? You're passing up some stops, aren't you?"

"A couple."

"Then how would he know that?"

"Maybe he doesn't. Maybe he'll just go to Memphis and wait."

"Or what?"

"What are you getting—oh, I see," Moses said. "You're implying that he's on this boat."

"Right."

"Then why hasn't he tried something onboard yet?"

"I don't know," Clint said, "but I think we should keep it in mind, don't you?"

"Maybe we should arm the crew anyway, even after our talk."

"Not with guns," Bixby said.

"What?" Moses turned.

"Sorry to butt in, boss, but I wouldn't give this crew guns. Most of them don't know how to use them."

"What would you arm them with, Mr. Bixby?"

"Knives," Captain Blowers said.

"Right," Bixby said. "Most of them carry them, anyway. Let's make sure they all have them. They know how to use *them*."

"Sounds like a good idea," Clint said.

"And clubs," Blowers said. "Every seaman knows how to use a club."

"The captain has a point," Bixby said.

"All right, then," Moses said, "we'll arm the crew with knives and clubs."

"What do we tell them?" Bixby asked.

"Tell them we're expecting trouble," Moses said. "That way they'll be ready for anything."

"Shall I take care of it?" Bixby asked.

"Yes, Mr. Bixby," Moses said, "you do that."

"Yes, sir." He turned to the captain. "Permission to leave the wheelhouse, Captain."

"Oh, all right," Blowers said, "but get your ass back here fast as you can."

"Yessir."

As Bixby left, Blowers looked at Moses and said, "Only decent pilot I ever worked with."

Moses had been watching Blowers for some time and decided that he was a very good captain, when he was sober—as he was now. That meant he gave Blowers's opinion about Bixby a lot of weight.

"What about the lad?" Moses asked, referring to the other pilot.

"He might learn," Blowers said, looking ahead of them. "He might . . . eventually."

"We'll leave you to your work, Captain," Moses said. "No need to push her. I know what she can do now."

"As you wish."

"Come on," Moses said to Clint.

"Where?"

"I think we should tell Laura and the other women what's going on so they don't wonder when they see all the armed men."

"How much do you want to tell them?" Clint asked.

"Just enough," Moses said. "Just enough."

FORTY-ONE

They decided that Clint would talk to Laura, while Moses spoke with Cinda. After that, Laura could tell her girls. Moses said he would talk to the new girls he'd hired to work the gaming room.

"How did they do last night, by the way?" Clint said. "I was a little too busy to notice."

"They did okay," Moses said. "One or two of the men made, uh, suggestions, but they explained that there were other girls onboard for that. There wasn't any trouble."

"That's good," Clint said. "About the game last night?"

"I haven't seen any of the other players yet today," Moses said.

"I noticed you let Ross play on credit."

"I know him," Moses said. "I think he's a good player, and I can trust him to pay up."

"He is a good player," Clint said, "but the others . . . if Anthony has so much money why don't you extend him credit?"

Moses laughed.

"Because I know him, too, that's why I make him pay up front."

They stopped when they reached the first upper deck.

"I'll find Cinda in the dining room. She's usually having lunch around this time."

"And Laura?"

"She'll be in her room."

"You keep pretty good track of your crew, don't you?"

"I do."

"Or is it just the female members?"

"Nope," Moses said, "everybody."

"How long before we reach Memphis?"

"If we were in a hurry it'd be about fourteen hours from Vicksburg to Memphis. We'll probably get there early in the morning."

"Maybe," Clint said, "you and I should stay aboard the *Queen* this time."

"And miss Memphis?"

"Why give somebody another chance at us?"

"If what you say is true and he's on the boat, then he'll just make his move here."

"That's okay," Clint said. "It's more confined here. There'll be too many places in Memphis where he could ambush us again. Do you have some reason you absolutely *have* to get off in Memphis?"

"No," Moses said, "I just *do* get off in every port. It's . . . well, it's like a superstition."

"Maybe it's time to break that particular superstition, Jack."

"I don't know," Moses said. "We'll see when we get there."

They split up then, Moses to talk to Cinda, and Clint to speak with Laura. Clint liked it that Moses kept his crew apprised of danger—even if he wasn't telling them exactly what the danger was.

FORTY-TWO

Laura was in her cabin, as Moses had predicted. Clint stepped inside and explained the situation to her. She was wearing a dressing gown that covered her up pretty well, but she folded her arms while she listened, which emphasized the full thrust of her large breasts.

"What do you want me and my girls to do?" she asked when he was done.

"I just want you to be aware that there might be trouble," Clint said. "When we dock in Memphis, just be alert."

"You think it's going to happen there?"

"Given what happened in Natchez, it wouldn't surprise me."

"Um," she said, "I heard about you being shot. I just haven't had a chance—are you all right?"

"I'm fine, Laura. Are you all right?"

She bit her bottom lip and said, "I thought I was. I guess I was foolish to sleep with him."

So that was it. She was still upset about Moses. She turned and walked toward the bed.

"Laura, he told me you knew it wouldn't last."

"I did know," she said. "That's why this is stupid. I thought I'd be able to do this."

"You can do it." He walked to her, took her by the

shoulders, and turned her around. "You're too smart to let a man do this to you. Forget about him. He's your boss and that's all. You'll meet another man, soon . . . and then another . . . keep using them, don't let them use you."

She looked up at him and smiled and pressed against him.

"How about you? Do you want to be used?"

He was very aware of her nearness now, her fragrance, her smooth skin, the way her firm breasts felt against his chest. He'd wondered from the start what she'd be like in bed, but then it was Cinda who came to him, and then Darla.

"Laura . . ."

She laughed and pushed away from him.

"I know. You have enough problems with Cinda and Darla."

"I don't have any problems," he said. "Cinda has the problem and she has to deal with it. As for Darla, she *knows* that nothing's going to happen."

"So then you are available?"

He stared at her as she undid the belt of her dressing gown. She dropped it to the floor and stood there naked. Her breasts were full and firm, her nipples large. Her hips were wide, her thighs almost chunky, and he knew when she turned her butt would be the same. She was a big woman, very sexy, and he felt himself responding.

"Laura . . ."

"It's up to you," she said. "Turn and walk out the door, or get undressed, Mr. Adams. I'll tell you a secret."

"What?" he asked, his mouth dry.

"Cinda beat me to your room by about a minute that first day," she said. "I thought about you for a long time."

"And I thought about you."

"Okay."

"But we're friends . . ."

"Let's stay friends," she said, moving close to him again, "*real* close friends." She took his hand and pressed it against one of her breasts, rubbing it there. Her nipple scraped his palm, and her flesh was smooth and hot. He squeezed her breast and her firmness excited him. She closed her eyes and her tongue flicked out to touch her bottom lip.

"Oh," he said, "what the hell . . ." and pulled her to him.

When he got off Laura's bed his legs felt weak. He'd been with her a couple of hours and there had been hardly any time when they *weren't* all over each other. Just a couple of hours with her had been almost as intense as the entire night with Darla. The experience with each woman had been different, but just as wonderful.

"Don't worry," she said as she watched him dress, "I'm not going to pine for you. We both know what this was."

"It was fun," he said.

"Mmm," she agreed, "and it was good."

He kissed her and moved to leave, reminding her to tell her girls about the trouble.

"Clint?" she said as he reached the door.

"Yes?"

"Thanks, I needed this."

"My pleasure," he said, and left.

When he came back on deck he noticed that they had slowed down considerably. He decided to lean on the rail and just enjoy the scenery that was going by. He wondered about his relationship with women, and how he usually avoided the kind of situation Moses was now involved in with Laura. He couldn't remember the last time he'd left a woman with bad feelings—except, of course, for Cinda. What he'd said to Laura was true, though. He hadn't done anything to Cinda; she'd managed to get upset all of her own accord about him getting shot. She was going to have to deal with it, and come to him about it.

Later he'd recall how preoccupied he was with women and curse himself for it. Now he heard a floorboard creak and turned in time to see a man almost on top of him. If he hadn't been daydreaming he would have noticed him a lot sooner.

The man had a club and swung it. Clint moved, avoiding being struck on the head, but the club struck his injured shoulder and he cried out in agony. Lights flashed before his eyes, and before he knew it he was tumbling over the side and splashing into the Mississippi. . . .

FORTY-THREE

The water was so cold it immediately cleared his head. He could see the *Biloxi Queen* continuing up the Mississippi and knew there was no point in crying out. He instinctively knew that he'd do better to save his breath for a swim to shore.

Using the *Queen* as a guide, he turned himself and began to swim toward the Mississippi side of the river rather than the Arkansas side. His shoulder ached but he knew he had to get out of the water as soon as he could. Even as he was swimming the river was taking him downstream, further from the *Queen*. He knew when he reached shore he was going to have to make his way to Memphis, and the river was taking him further from there, as well.

His concern was for J. P. Moses. With him gone Moses would be on his own in Memphis. He'd been right about there being a man onboard the boat, and now he thought it was likely that the man had help waiting in Memphis.

He kept his eyes on the shoreline and swam as hard as he could. He didn't seem to be getting any closer, but he knew that was an illusion. Soon his feet would touch bottom and he'd walk up on shore and . . . what?

And he'd be totally lost.

• • •

Joe Harding cursed. Again he'd made a mistake. He had wanted to kill Adams and then dump him overboard. It was possible that he would drown in the Mississippi, but there was no way he could be sure. He was going to have to move very quickly when they got to Memphis, more quickly than he had planned. He only hoped that his men would be ready.

J. P. Moses entered the wheelhouse. Both Captain Blowers and Mr. Bixby turned to look at him.

"Have either of you seen Clint?"

Blowers shook his head.

Bixby said, "No, sir, not since he was here with you earlier."

"I can't find him anywhere," Moses said.

"Could he be—" Bixby asked, then stopped.

"Could he be where?" Moses asked.

"Excuse me, sir, but could he be with one of the women?"

"That's a definite possibility, I guess," Moses said.

"You could try knocking on some doors."

"That could prove embarrassing," Moses said. "I guess I'll just give him some time and then look for him again. I'll be down in the gaming room, Bixby, getting things started."

"Yes, sir."

Moses left the wheelhouse. If Clint was with a woman, he wondered which one. Cinda? Darla? Or one of the others? Well, whichever one it was he hoped his friend was having a good time.

Clint reached shore, pulled himself from the water's edge, and collapsed, exhausted. Although he had had very little opportunity to swim, he was a strong swimmer. Fighting the current of the Mississippi, however, had taken a lot out of him—and it was dark. He had no idea what time it was. He knew he couldn't afford to waste time, but he was going to have to rest just a little bit before he tried to walk. His shoulder was aching from the blow he'd received, and he knew he was probably bleeding from the existing wound, but somehow he was going to have to find out where the hell he was, how far from Memphis he was, *and* he was going to have to try to find some transportation there.

One way or another he had to beat the *Biloxi Queen* there to warn J. P. Moses. The attack on him was proof that something big was going to happen in Memphis, and he wanted to be there for it.

FORTY-FOUR

The games were in full swing, including the private poker game in the corner, and still Clint hadn't shown up. What was even more odd was that all of the women were working. At one point Moses had gone down to Clint's cabin and let himself in. Maybe he'd spent so much time with one of the women that he had worn himself out, but the cabin was empty.

Now he was worried.

"Where's Mr. Adams tonight, Mr. Moses?" Eric asked.

"I'm wondering that myself, Eric," Moses said. "Have you seen him in the last few hours?"

"No, sir."

"Not even just before you came to work?"

"Uh, no, sir." Eric sounded very guilty about something.

"What were you doing just before work, Eric?"

"Well, sir, I . . ."

"Come on, spit it out."

"Uh, I was with Marianne, sir."

That meant Clint hadn't been with her. Maybe he should ask all of the girls who saw him last.

"Okay, Eric," he said, "if you see Clint tell him I'm looking for him, okay? Hang on to him."

"Do you think something might have happened to him, sir?"

"Yes, Eric," Moses said, "that's what I'm afraid of."

Moses left the gaming room and stared over the side at the swirling waters of the Big Muddy. For all the years he'd known Clint he didn't even know if his friend could swim or not. If someone had dumped him overboard . . .

Had the Mississippi taken from him someone else he cared about?

Clint staggered away from the Mississippi, fixing on a light he could see in the distance. As with the shoreline, he seemed to be getting no closer while he walked, and then suddenly there was a house. He lurched to the door and banged on it.

"Land sakes," a woman was saying as she opened the door, but she stopped when Clint toppled into the house and fell at her feet. "Pa!" she shouted. "We got another poor soul fell off one of them riverboats!"

The old couple's names were Jed and Sally Overland, and they said that two or three times a month some poor soul fell into the river, swam ashore, and knocked on their door.

"Most in worse shape than you," Sally said.

Clint was working on a cup of Sally's strong black coffee, sitting wrapped in a blanket. His gun was on the table in front of him; he'd quickly stripped it and dried it under their watchful eye. Jed knew that a man who took that good care of his gun used it quite a bit.

"I appreciate your help," Clint said. "I'm sorry to be a bother."

"You're no bother," Sally said.

"What's the nearest town?"

"That'd be Whitehaven," Jed said. "It's about ten miles away."

"Am I in Mississippi or Tennessee?"

"Tennessee."

"How far from Memphis?"

"Well," Jed said, rubbing his grizzled jaw, "Memphis is about fifteen miles from Whitehaven."

That meant he'd have to travel twenty-five miles.

"And how far from here?"

"Oh, from here Memphis is almost as close as Whitehaven. I'd say about eleven, twelve miles."

Clint didn't know how long it had been since he fell off the *Queen*. He had no idea how long it had taken him to swim to shore and then walk to the Overland house.

"I've got to get to Memphis as quickly as I can," he said. "Do you have a horse I can use?"

"Ain't got but one," Jed Overland said, "and we need her."

"Jed," Clint said, "I really need to get to Memphis quickly. It's a matter of life and death."

"Whose?"

"A friend of mine," Clint said. "His name's J. P. Moses—"

"*Mister* Moses?" Jed asked.

"That's right."

"You fell off'n his boat? The *Dead Man's Chance*?"

"He has a second boat, the *Biloxi Queen*, and this is the first time it's going upriver—and I didn't fall off, I was pushed."

"That how your shoulder got banged up?" Sally asked.

"Yes, ma'am."

"You really oughta lemme look at that for ya."

"It's okay, really," Clint said. "It's . . . it's not bleeding anymore.'' It was still throbbing like hell, though. "Jed? Can you help me?''

"Is it Mr. Moses who's in trouble?" Jed asked.

"Yes, it is.''

"Well, then, I can take you to Memphis.''

"If you give me the horse I can—''

"You gotta know the way," Sally said, "or you'll get lost for sure. Jed knows the way.''

"I'll hitch up the buckboard," Jed said. "You probably shouldn't be riding, anyway, as banged up as you are.''

"And tired," Sally said. "Lord knows anybody who ever fell in that river and got out is dog tired.''

"I am tired. . . .'' he admitted.

"Then you get that there gun put back together," Jed said, standing up, "and I'll get the buckboard.''

FORTY-FIVE

Jed told Clint that there was a bend in the Mississippi right near them that increased the distance to Memphis.

"We're going in a straight line."

"So we'll beat them there?" Clint asked hopefully.

"I don't know about that," Jed said. "I know the way, but it's dark and we can't go real fast. If I had to guess, I'd say we'd get there about the same time."

"Daylight?"

"Daylight."

Clint hoped that would be good enough.

Moses had checked with all the women, and no one had seen Clint for hours. Laura even told him that Clint had been with her earlier, but she hadn't seen him since. Everyone was now worried.

Gaming was over for the day. The only people who were glad Clint hadn't been around were the men he'd played poker with the night before. In his absence Bruce Stilwell had cleaned up.

The gaming room was empty except for Moses, Eric, Laura, Cinda, and Darla. Everyone else had gone to bed. The only others who were awake were crew who were on duty.

"You figure he went overboard, don't you?" Laura asked.

"Yeah, I do," Moses said.

"Who'd do that?" Darla asked.

"Clint said somebody was onboard," Moses said.

"Who?" Eric asked.

"I don't know," Moses said. "It'd have to be somebody who was keeping an eye on Clint, me, or both. Did anyone notice somebody like that?"

"Oh, my . . ." Cinda started.

"What?" Moses asked. "Cinda, do you know something?"

"The man," she said.

"What man?"

"The man who kept losing at my table because he wasn't paying attention."

"Maybe he was looking at the girls," Moses said.

"No," she said, "I remember distinctly he took a hit on nineteen because he was looking toward the bar—you and Clint were at the bar."

"What was his name?" Moses asked.

"I don't know his name," Cinda said. "The players don't all give me their names."

"He didn't give you his name?" Moses asked. "He didn't make a play for you?"

"No," Cinda said.

"That's suspicious right there," Eric said.

Cinda graced Eric with a smile.

"We've got to find this man," Moses said. "Cinda? You'll know him if you see him again?"

"Definitely."

"Can we help?" Darla asked.

"No," Moses said. "Cinda and I will have to do this.

The rest of you go back to your cabins.''

Darla and Laura grumbled, but they did as they were told.

''Mr. Moses,'' Eric said, ''I want to help.''

Moses looked the young man up and down for a moment, then said, ''All right, but you do exactly as I tell you.''

''Yes, sir.''

''We've got to find this man before we reach Memphis, and that's only a few hours away.''

''And if we don't?'' Cinda asked.

''If we don't,'' Moses said, ''it'll be daylight, and he'll have help waiting there.''

''Let's get to it, then,'' Eric said.

''We'll go cabin by cabin,'' Moses said, ''and Cinda, you sing out as soon as you see him. I'll take care of the rest.'' Moses touched the gun in his belt.

''Do I need a gun?'' Eric asked.

''Do you know how to use one?''

''Well . . .''

''Eric?''

''No.''

''Get a club then,'' Moses said, ''you'll back me up with that.''

''Yes, sir.''

''Meet us on deck in ten minutes.''

''Right.''

''Do you think he's dead?'' Cinda asked. ''Clint, I mean?''

''Clint's got more lives than a cat,'' Moses said.

''I hope so.''

Moses only hoped that Clint wasn't up to his ninth life.

FORTY-SIX

As the sun rose Clint rubbed both hands over his face vigorously. Jed had offered him dry clothes, but he hadn't wanted to take the time to change. His had dried, but they felt grimy, and his skin itched. None of that mattered, though. Along the way he had fired his gun once just to test it, and it worked. *That* was what mattered.

"You take damned good care of that thing," Jed had said.

"Yes, I do," Clint said, reloading.

"You a gunslick?"

"No."

"But you know how to use one, don't ya?"

"I know how."

Jed had let it go at that.

"How much farther, Jed?"

"Not far," Jed said. "We can start to go faster now that daylight is comin'."

With that said he snapped the reins at his horse, but the animal was old and couldn't manage much more in the way of speed. If Clint had tried to ride the animal he probably would have killed him.

Also, the trail they were on wasn't much of a trail. There was lots of brush around them, and Clint couldn't even see how Jed knew the way in the dark, but apparently he did—at least, he hoped he did.

"We need to get to the docks, Jed."

"We'll get there, young feller," Jed said. "We'll get there."

But they needed to get there in *time*!

"It's daylight," Eric said.

Moses almost snapped that he knew that, but he held his tongue. They'd knocked on most of the cabin doors on the *Queen*. Some of the people were very irate at being awakened, but Moses couldn't take the time to explain. If there was a man in the cabin, Cinda took a look at him, but so far she hadn't recognized anyone.

They kept on.

Harding knew what was going on. He heard some commotion down the hall and slipped from his room to take a look. He saw Moses, the blackjack dealer, and the bartender talking to someone in one of the cabins, and it didn't take a genius to figure out that they were looking for him. They'd missed Adams, figured that something had happened, and now they were looking for him. The only thing he didn't know was if they somehow knew what he looked like. Then he figured that out, too. He'd been losing at the blackjack dealer's table because he wasn't paying attention. The only reason she'd be along was to identify him.

He didn't go back to his cabin. Instead he went to find someplace to hide himself until the boat reached Memphis.

A crewman came and found Moses, sent by the captain to tell him they were approaching Memphis.

"All right, tell him I'll be there."

"What happened to him?" Cinda asked.

"He caught on."

"How?"

"I don't know," Moses said, "but he's hiding on the boat somewhere."

"Should we break into the cabins where no one answered?" Eric asked. "Maybe he's hiding inside."

"Maybe," Moses said, "but we don't have time. Eric, get some help and rouse the whole crew. Tell them we may have some trouble in Memphis."

"What about guns?"

"Tell the men who have them and know how to use them to bring them."

"Yes, sir."

"What should I do?" Cinda asked.

"Go to your cabin and stay there. You'll be safe."

"A-are you sure?"

"Nothing will happen to you and the other girls," Moses said. "These men will be after me."

"W-what if they try to sink the boat?"

"It's easier to kill me than sink the boat," Moses said. "Besides, there are two possibilities as to who's behind this, and neither man is going to want to sink the *Queen*."

"Are you su—"

"Go to your cabin, Cinda!" he snapped. "Don't come out, any of you, until I send some crew for you, or come for you myself."

"A-all right."

As Cinda obeyed, Moses wondered where the son of a bitch was hiding. There were so many damned hiding places on a riverboat. . . .

If Clint Adams was dead, he wanted this son of a bitch bad!

• • •

"What's that up ahead?" Clint asked. He saw some buildings through the brush.

"That there's Memphis."

At last! But would they be in time?

FORTY-SEVEN

Eric not only roused the crew and gave them Moses's instructions, but told them what was going on, and that they had a man who was hiding on the boat.

"We've got to find him," Eric finished.

"How?" a crewman asked. "We don't know what he looks like."

"Those of us without positions can start looking," Eric said. "All we need to do is find a man who looks like he's hiding and hold him. It doesn't matter if we know what he looks like or not. Come on, we've got to do this for Mr. Moses."

"You heard him, men," the crewman said. "Let's go."

Moses was in the wheelhouse as the *Biloxi Queen* pulled into dock. It was the safest place for him. If anyone tried to board the boat, they'd have to go through a lot of crew to get to him. Also, from up here he'd have easy shots at them. In addition to that, this gave him the best vantage point of the dock, so he could see trouble if it was coming.

On the dock five men were secreting themselves anywhere they could, waiting for a signal from Joe Harding aboard the *Queen*. Their instructions were clear. Get to J. P.

Moses and kill anyone who got in their way. Since this was their business, the men didn't think they'd have any trouble getting through the crew, no matter how many there were. It was their experience that men who were not prepared to kill fled at the first sign of a dead man. They'd probably only have to kill two or three and the crew would open up like the Red Sea and leave them a path to Moses.

From behind them the men heard the sound of a buckboard but paid it no mind.

''There's the signal,'' one of them said, as the gangplank was lowered. ''Let's go.''

Clint was off the buckboard even before it stopped.

''Hey—'' Jed shouted, but he ignored the older man and started running toward the *Queen*.

''Stay inside!'' Moses instructed both Blowers and Bixby. He didn't need his captain or best pilot getting killed. As he stepped outside he decided he needed to hire more crewmen who could handle guns.

Moses saw two things happening at once. Five men suddenly burst from hiding with guns in their hands and charged the *Queen*. Second, a man leapt from a moving buckboard behind them and also ran toward the boat.

The man looked like a dirty, disheveled Clint Adams.

Moses took the easiest course of action.

''Raise that gangplank!'' he shouted.

As the five men converged on the gangplank it suddenly disappeared, pulled back onboard the *Queen*.

''Hey!'' one of them shouted. ''Now what?''

Before any of them could answer, Clint Adams shouted from behind them, "Put up your guns!"

The five men froze.

"One man," one of them said.

"Let's take him," another said.

As they turned, both Clint Adams and J. P. Moses fired, and when they did, every other gun onboard did, as well.

FORTY-EIGHT

"Goddamn it," Clint said, "why don't you hire some men who can shoot?"

"I was thinking that myself."

Both men looked down at the bullet-riddled remains of the five men. Clint had killed one, Moses another, and then the barrage had started from the boat. Clint had to run for cover because the crew were such bad shots.

"They almost killed me."

"Hell," Moses said, "haven't you proved how many lives you've got? You got away from the river."

"I got away from it," he said, then shrugged. "The Mississippi isn't so tough."

Moses put his hand on his friend's good shoulder.

"It's good to see you—even if you do look like shit."

"Mr. Moses?"

They both turned and looked up at the top of the gangplank. Two men were holding one man between them, and Eric was behind them.

"Mr. Moses?" Eric called again. "We found him."

"What's the meaning of this?" the captive man asked.

"Bring him down," Moses yelled, "and get Cinda."

The two crewmen wrestled the man down the gangplank to face Moses and Clint.

"I don't know him," Moses said. "Do you?"

180

"No," Clint said.

"What's going on here?" the man demanded.

"What's your name?"

"I'm not answering any questions. Tell these men to let me go."

"In due time, mister," Moses said. "If we're wrong I'll apologize, but if we're right you're going to have to face this man." Moses indicated Clint, who smiled unpleasantly at the man.

"I can swim," he said to the man, "but I hate doing it with my clothes on."

"I don't know what—"

"Clint!" Cinda shouted, coming down the gangplank. Behind her came Darla, Laura, and the other girls, even the new girls.

"Are you all right?" Darla asked.

"I'm fine," Clint said. "Just a little dirty, and a little tired."

"Cinda," Moses asked, "is this your bad blackjack player?"

"That's him," she said. "He was more interested in watching you two than watching his cards."

The man pressed his lips together.

"You've got two choices," Clint said. "Talk or swim."

"I can swim," the man said defiantly.

"With your hands tied?" Moses asked.

The man's eyes widened.

"You wouldn't!"

"Bind his hands," Moses said.

"Yes, sir," one of the crewmen said.

"Wait, wait . . ." Joe Harding cried out. "What do you want to know?"

Moses looked at Clint and smiled.

"He's all yours," Clint said. "I need a bath."

"You're getting soft in your old age," Moses said.

"Ultimately, he was after you and your boat," Clint said. "I figured you deserved to have him."

"Thanks."

They were in the dining salon, and Clint was wolfing down a hot breakfast. Swimming was hungry work.

"What did you do with him?" he asked.

"Turned him over to the law."

"And what are they going to do?"

"They're going to have a talk with Cole Aldridge."

Harding had confessed to being hired by Aldridge to sabotage the *Biloxi Queen* any way he could, short of sinking it. He figured the best way was to kill the owner.

"That won't accomplish much," Clint said. "Not with his money."

"It'll keep him off my back for a while."

"He's liable to be a thorn in your side for a long time to come."

"I don't know why he doesn't like me," Moses said.

"What about Masters?"

"I don't know," Moses said. "I guess I'll deal with him if he pops up again. My guess is he's still in Biloxi, looking for a new boat."

"Did you take care of Jed Overland for me?"

"I did," Moses said. "I gave him a very nice reward for helping you and me."

"Good, thanks. When do we get under way again?"

"You staying on? After all this?"

"I'm not going to waste a swim in the Mississippi," Clint said. "Besides, I was looking forward to seeing St.

Paul, and some of the smaller cities along the way."

"The rest of the trip might be uneventful," Moses said, "except for the usual."

"The usual?"

"You know," Moses said, "women and gambling."

Clint grinned, poured himself some more hot coffee, and said, "That's what I'm counting on."

Watch for

SIX FOR THE MONEY

186th novel in the exciting GUNSMITH series
from Jove

Coming in June!